The Jerry McNeal Series

Ghostly Guidance

(A Paranormal Snapshot)

By Sherry A. Burton

The Jerry McNeal Series

Ghostly Guidance

By Sherry A. Burton

The Jerry McNeal Series: Ghostly Guidance
Copyright 2022

by Sherry A. Burton
Published by Dorry Press
Edited and Formatted by BZHercules.com
Cover by Laura J. Prevost
@laurajprevostphotography

ISBN: 978-1-951386-10-8

For more information on the author and her works, please see www.SherryABurton.com

To all the working dogs and those K-9s who have lost their lives while protecting others.

Public Safety Dogs, Inc. is a nonprofit 501(c)(3) organization. Originally founded as Canines for Kids, Inc. in 2003 by Mike Craig and Linda Dunn, Public Safety Dogs trains a variety of scent dogs and donates the dogs, all of their equipment, and their handlers' training to Law Enforcement Agencies and Fire Departments across the United States. To follow Public Safety Dogs on Facebook:

www.facebook.com/publicsafetydogs

To learn more about Public Safety Dogs, check out this website:

www.publicsafetydogs.com

To my hubby, thanks for helping me stay in the writing chair.

To my mom, who insisted I keep the dog in the series.

To my editor, Beth, for allowing me to keep my voice.

To Laura, for EVERYTHING you do to keep me current in both my covers and graphics.

To my beta readers for giving the books an early read.

To my proofreader, Latisha Rich, for the extra set of eyes.

To my fans, for the continued support.

Lastly, to my "voices," thank you for all the incredible ideas!

Table of Contents

Chapter One

Jerry poured himself a cup of coffee, resisting an urge to football-kick the cat who was currently purring incessantly against his leg. He palmed his coffee cup, dodging the feline as he walked to the table to read his mail. Tired of being ignored, the cat jumped onto the table, voicing his need to be fed.

"Stay off the table, Cat," Jerry said, calling him by name and scooping him onto the floor.

Not one to be dismissed, Cat jumped up once more as Jerry tapped the phone number into his cell phone. When he'd finished dialing, Jerry used his free hand to place the cat back on the floor. Incensed, the cat sat staring at Jerry, its tail whipping from side to side as if contemplating his next move.

"This had better be worth waking up for," came a groggy voice on the other end of the phone.

Jerry instantly regretted calling at such an early hour. He debated hanging up but knew the person on the other end already had his number. Hoping to avoid confrontation, he opted for a formal introduction. "This is Trooper First Class

Jerry McNeal in Chambersburg, Pennsylvania; I'm calling in regard to a letter I received."

"Mr. McNeal, I sent that letter weeks ago." The woman sighed heavily into the phone. "I didn't think you were going to call."

Jerry picked up the letter and scanned the signature – April Buchanan. He could make up an excuse or just tell her the truth – that he got so many letters from people claiming to either be like him or wanting him to use his gift to help them out of their financial bind, that he hated opening his mail. He opted instead for a simple apology. "I'm sorry it's taken me so long to get in touch."

"I'm sorry. I know you must be busy. I'm just grateful that you took the time to call. Hang on, and I'll wake Maxine."

"I apologize for the early morning call. I can call back this evening if you'd prefer."

"No!... Please don't hang up. It will just take me a moment to get up the stairs. Max will be happy to hear from you. Lord knows she needs to talk to someone who understands."

Jerry smiled a triumphant smile as Cat once again decided to weave in and around his legs, purring and covering his pants with orange fur. Never being around a cat before, he'd quickly grown wise to the cat's wicked ways of shedding hair all over the legs of his neatly pressed uniform. After the first few times of playing dodge-the-cat, he decided it was much easier to dress in sweatpants until time to change into his work uniform. "So, this doesn't run in the family?"

"Heavens, no. Is that how it normally works?"

Hell if I know. "Just making conversation, ma'am." Actually, if he could establish a family connection, it would give Max's intuitions credibility.

"Have any of her premonitions come true?"

"Oh yes, all the time. Why, just last night, she blessed me before I even sneezed."

"I wouldn't exactly call that a premonition." Jerry resisted rolling his eyes.

"I sneezed a second later. What would you call it?"

"Maybe I should wait to speak to Max." *Or hang up and let you go back to bed.* Jerry could hear muffled talking on the other end of the phone.

"Hello?" The voice sounded much like that of her mother. "Trooper McNeal, is it really you?"

"Yeah, Max, it's me. Sorry it took so long to call. Your mom tells me you've had some disturbing dreams."

"Yes, sir."

"How about you tell me about them." While he'd hoped they were just nightmares, his own radar currently told him there was more to it.

"There's not much to tell. Everything is still

3

blurry in my dream. I see a lady and know she's going to die."

"Do you know this lady?"

"I don't think so."

"Are you sure?"

"She feels familiar, but I don't think it's anyone I know."

"I think you need to give it some time."

"How much time?"

"I don't know."

"What do you mean you don't know? Mom said you could help."

Jerry could feel her anxiety rising and took in a calming breath. "Max, I'm not trying to brush you off. I'll do everything in my power to help. What I'm saying is you need to be sure."

"How?"

"Keep a notebook beside your bed. Revisit your dream. Write everything down the moment it comes to you. Think back to see if you might have watched something on TV or read anything in the paper that could be influencing your dreams."

"Can't I just call the police?"

"You can. The problem is getting them to believe you."

"Then you can call them for me. Tell them what I told you."

Please don't ask me to do that.

"Do you believe me?" she asked when he didn't answer. He could hear the tremble in her voice.

"I want to," he answered as honestly as he could.

"But you don't."

He could tell she was crying. "Max, I know you believe it, and it feels very real to you. But you're not the first person to have reached out to me. People call, send letters, stop me on the street. At first, I was happy to have found kindred spirits and so I believed them all. A few were legitimate, some a complete farce, and others were just simply people having recurring dreams, much like when people get songs stuck in their heads."

"If I do nothing, someone is going to die." This time, her voice held conviction.

"It would be easier for you and the police if you knew who that someone was. That's why I need you to start keeping a journal."

"I can almost see her."

"That's good. Give it some time, Max. Maybe it'll come to you. Even then, you may have trouble getting people to listen to you."

"Because I'm a kid?"

Partly. "Because people have a difficult time believing things they can't understand."

"Do people believe you?"

"A few. But that didn't happen overnight." His grandmother had the gift, but it had skipped over his mother and younger brother. His father had always shied away from discussing it. Some of the guys he worked with seemed to accept it; others held him at arm's length, making the odd joke about him knowing things about their personal business. Sergeant Seltzer was a believer, which helped when Jerry needed to go off to follow a feeling.

"Jerry?"

"Yeah, Max?"

"I hope I can figure out what I'm supposed to know before it's too late."

"Me too, kid."

"Jerry?"

"Yeah, Max?"

"I'm sorry about your dog."

Jerry stiffened in his chair. He'd not told a soul about what happened during the blizzard. "My dog?"

"I'm sorry." She sniffed.

He decided to rephrase the question. "What about my dog?"

"I thought you knew."

"Knew what?"

"Your dog is dead."

"Max. What does my dog look like?"

She laughed a nervous giggle. "Is this some kind of exercise?"

"I just want to see how accurate you can perceive things." He spoke softly, trying to put her at ease.

"A German shepherd. He's beautiful, by the way. Or was."

"Go on," Jerry encouraged.

"Brown with black markings on his face. His ears go straight up, and he's missing part of one. A gun. He got shot, but there's more. Gun – is that his name, or is it Gunner...his ear...a fight...Jerry, did someone bite off your dog's ear?" Her voice was incredulous.

Jerry stared into the phone. *The girl's good. She's going to need help. How are you going to help her when you can't even help yourself?*

"Are you there, Jerry?"

"I'm here, Max. The dog's name is Gunter, and he's not my dog. He's a police dog. Or he was."

"It's weird."

"What's weird?"

"I know he's dead. But I feel like he's alive."

"What if I told you you're right?"

"Which one?"

"Both."

"I don't understand."

"Gunter is dead, but I saw him."

"You saw him get killed?"

"I saw him after he was dead and buried." *Great, she's going to go to school and blab it to all her friends.*

"Cool!"

"Max, I haven't told anyone except you about that."

"Why not?"

"When you're a kid, and you walk into a

police station and tell someone you're having dreams of someone getting murdered, they're going to treat you like a kid. I'm a police officer. If I go telling people I see ghosts, they're going to have me committed."

"Even though they know what you can do?"

"Remember what I told you about people being scared of what they can't explain."

"Will it ever get easier for us?"

I've asked myself that a million times. Not wanting to dash her hopes, he said the only thing that came to mind. "Kids can be cruel – be careful who you tell. Some will think it's cool, but others will expect things from you that you might not be able to deliver."

"I've already found that out." Her voice cracked. "It kind of sucks sometimes."

"It sure does." Jerry watched as Cat, having given up on getting his food from Jerry, decided to go straight to the source – jumping onto the counter and pawing open the cabinet that contained the cat food. "Listen, I've got to be going. Keep my number and let me know if I can answer any more questions. And Max?"

"Yeah, Jerry."

"If you want me to call your police station for you, I will. Just let me know when you're ready."

"Does that mean you believe me?"

"You're the only one that knows about the dog."

"It must be pretty cool having a ghost dog."

"I don't have him. He just showed up at the accident scene and helped me find a lady that probably wouldn't have been found if he wasn't there."

"Cool!"

"Yeah, it was pretty cool." He smiled.

"Like Christmas."

"What?"

"The lady's name – Holly, it sounds like Christmas."

Damn, she's good. "Max?"

"Yeah, Jerry."

"Remind me never to play poker with you."

"That's what my dad says."

"Have a good day, Max."

"You too, Jerry. And don't worry about the dog. He'll be back."

That's exactly what I'm worried about, Jerry thought, clicking off the phone. The second he placed the phone on the table, Cat jumped up, sniffing the phone.

"You're not going to win," Jerry said, placing him onto the floor once more. "I have many things in my life that I can't control, but keeping you off my table isn't one of them. I will win this battle."

Cat meowed his answer, which to Jerry meant "challenge accepted."

Chapter Two

Jerry scanned the parking lot of the state police post, saw Manning's lime-green pickup, and turned the opposite direction. That Manning was here didn't come as a surprise – Sergeant Seltzer had told Jerry of his impending return the previous day. What did come as a surprise was that Manning was early. While he didn't dislike the man, Jerry had hoped to be on the road well before he arrived. He parked his truck, started toward the building, and hesitated when his inner radar told him he wasn't alone. Though he couldn't see the dog, the hairs on his arms told him he was near.

Maybe Manning being here wasn't a bad thing after all. Perhaps the dog was confused. After all, Gunter had showed up when Jerry was forced to drive Manning's SUV during the snowstorm. It all made sense now; the dog wasn't attached to him – it was attached to the SUV. That was why he hadn't seen the K-9 in the days since the accident. *What a relief.* "Okay, dog, let's take a walk. It's time for you to attach yourself to someone who actually cares about you."

"Yo, McNeal, what are you doing here?" Manning asked the second Jerry entered the building. Manning's cubicle was nowhere near the front door, making it obvious the man had been waiting for him.

"Last I saw, I still work here." Jerry resisted the temptation to look to see if the dog was visible. The lack of emotion on Manning's chiseled face told him what he needed to know. He started toward the back, pausing when Manning blocked his way. Jerry caught a glimpse of white hair, saw Sergeant Seltzer looking in their direction, and gave a subtle nod, letting his boss know he had things under control.

"I see the psychic convention's in town. I guess I figured you'd be there with the others."

"Some of us have to have real jobs," Jerry quipped.

"Wait. Say it isn't true. You're going to stand there and tell me you don't believe in that crap." Manning snorted.

I don't know what I believe. "Let it go, Manning."

Anger flashed in Manning's eyes. "No, I'm not going to let it go. You go around like a cowboy on a white horse saving the day, and you think you're the only one? So I'm to believe you've cornered the market on the psychic shit. It's just you, and all other psychics are frauds."

Not all of them. Jerry could tell by the set of

Manning's shoulders he was looking for an argument and had a pretty good idea why he had singled him out – he needed someone to blame for what had happened to his partner and had decided that someone should be Jerry. No shock; Jerry was used to being the scapegoat. He'd been nowhere near the scene when the dog got shot. And therein lay the problem. "Step aside, Manning."

"Look at you hiding behind that uniform. I see you for what you really are. You know you ain't nothing but a damn coward." Manning grabbed him by the arm as he tried to pass. "Always running away. Couldn't cut it as a Marine, so you joined the State Police. The reason you aren't at the convention is you know you can't cut it as a psychic either."

Instinct took over. Jerry jerked his arm out of Manning's grip, pushed him against the wall, and leaned in close. "What's your beef, Manning?"

"My beef is you. You use your …whatever it is…to help everyone but those close to you. Maybe if you quit running when things get a bit tough, you could focus your energy on what matters."

Jerry narrowed his eyes, hoping Manning hadn't seen he'd touched a nerve. "Yeah, and what's that?"

"Family. Me, your fellow officers, my freaking dog. Maybe if you would have let us in, you would've felt something the night Gunter got shot." Manning's voice cracked as he said the dog's name.

So it was true. Manning did blame him. It made perfect sense; why would he want to blame the whack-job that had fired the gun that actually killed the dog. *Shit? Is that why the dog's haunting me? Because he blames me for getting him killed? Easy, Jerry, you're losing it.* "I'm sorry your dog's dead." Jerry released the man.

"He was more than just a dog." Manning was calmer now. "He saved my life."

"I know," Jerry replied, wishing he could tell him of the dog's latest heroics.

"I heard about the crash on Route 30 the other day," Manning said as Jerry stepped around him. "That was a good save."

Manning was talking about the accident involving a very intriguing photographer named Holly and a snowplow. What he didn't know was that the dog he was mourning had been instrumental in finding the woman whose car had veered off the side of the road during the blizzard and was buried at the bottom of the ravine. While Jerry's gift had led him to the accident, it had not led him to Holly, who would have died if not for the dog. Over the last couple of days, he'd contemplated telling the man, but any hope of convincing him now would be construed as a way for Jerry to ease his conscience. Besides, what would he say? *Sorry you miss your dog, but if it's any consolation, the dog's now a ghost and seems to like me more than you.* Jerry decided to take the easy way out. "Thanks."

"We good?" Manning asked, moving aside.

"Good as we always were." While Jerry didn't see the dog, he held his arm to his side, spreading his fingers, giving the sign for stay, hoping Gunter would see it and know to stay with his old partner.

"Problem?" Seltzer asked when Jerry went into the sergeant's office.

Jerry shrugged. "He blames me for not saving his dog."

"Want me to talk to him?"

"You talk to him, you're going to have to talk to Jackson as well. He stopped me the other day."

"Jackson's not sore about the dog too, is he?"

"He wanted the winning lottery numbers."

"What'd he say when you told him you don't know?" Seltzer leaned forward in his chair. "You don't know, do you?"

"If I did, I wouldn't be here."

"It would solve a lot of problems," Seltzer said, running a hand through his white hair.

"Me not being here?"

"You knowing the lottery numbers. I wonder why that is?"

"I'm not sure I'm following you," Jerry replied.

"Why people like you can know some things and not know others. So, what are you going to do about Manning?" Seltzer asked, not waiting for an answer to the previous question.

Jerry waited for Seltzer to take a drink of coffee. "I was thinking about telling him his dog's a ghost."

Seltzer spit coffee from his nose. " Jesus, McNeal, you can't go around joking like that."

Jerry stared at the dog who'd materialized and now lay just in front of Seltzer's desk.

His boss's eyes grew wide as he stood and peeked over the desk. Blowing out a breath of air, the man sat back down. "You had me there for a moment."

Jerry looked to the now empty spot where the dog had been lying just a second before. *No need to bring him in on your little delusion, Jerry.* He smiled. "Just trying to keep you on your toes, sir."

"More like trying to send me to an early grave. Can you imagine the press if something like that were to get out? Might help with the budget, though."

"How's that?"

"Because now we have to fund another K-9. Do you think they really exist?"

"K-9s?"

"No, ghosts. You're wired into that stuff. Have you ever seen one?"

Jerry slid a glance to Gunter, who'd not only materialized but now looked at him with his head tilted to the side as if waiting to hear his answer. He focused his gaze on Seltzer. "I guess if I can know when something's going to happen before it does, then I'd have to say ghosts are plausible."

"But you've never seen one yourself?"

Easy, Jerry, time to tread lightly. "Sir, I have so much shit floating around in my head, it's hard at times to know what's real and what isn't."

"Yeah, I guess it would be at that," Seltzer agreed.

"Hey, about that K-9. I have a friend in North Carolina who trains dogs and donates them to police. I believe he only does search and rescue, but I can reach out to him if you'd like." Jerry hoped Seltzer would say yes, as it would give him an opportunity to ask some questions of his own.

"Donate, you say? And they're already trained?"

"Highly trained. Mike knows his stuff and has plenty of references."

"See what you can find out and get back to me. Anything else?" Seltzer asked when Jerry made no move to leave.

"I may need you to make a call for me."

"Go on." Seltzer leaned back in his chair.

"There's this girl." Seltzer cocked an eyebrow, and Jerry shook his head. "Max is a kid. Her mother sent me a letter asking me to speak to the girl."

"This one for real?"

"I'm afraid so."

"You say that like it's a bad thing."

"She needs a mentor."

"So mentor her."

"You make it sound easy."

"I won't pretend to know what it's like, but I know you and know you're not going to lead anyone astray."

"Not on purpose."

"So, who do you need me to call?"

"No one yet. Max doesn't have enough information." Jerry blew out a frustrated sigh. "She has dreams about someone being murdered, only that's pretty much all she knows. And that she thinks it's a woman."

"Pretty thin."

"That's what I told her."

"What makes you so sure she's legit?"

Because she knew about the dog. "Because when I was talking to her, she picked up on Holly."

"Who?"

"Ms. Wood, the woman from the blizzard."

"Why would she pick up on her?"

Because I was thinking about her at the time. Don't go there, Jerry. He shrugged. "I talked to the girl right after the accident."

"Let me know if you need me to help." Seltzer pulled out a pack of gum, removed a stick, and returned the pack to the drawer. "You want to go further out in the state today? I was thinking to send you over to Hershey. Might give you a chance to check in on Ms. Wood."

That was the thing about Seltzer; he believed in Jerry – so much so, he allowed him to choose where he wanted to patrol. Probably because Jerry never took advantage of the man's generosity. Jerry started to shake his head; ever since Manning had mentioned the psychic convention, the hairs on the back of Jerry's neck were tingling. But whatever he was feeling wasn't demanding his immediate attention.

Jerry looked at the dog, who was lying with his head resting on his front paws. "I think that'll be okay."

"Let me know if anything changes. And, McNeal, if that girl's as good as you think she is, you tell her to come see me when she's ready to go to work."

"I'll be sure to pass it along." Jerry stood, and the dog instantly joined him at his side. Jerry made it a point to walk past Manning's cubicle in hopes of getting the dog to stay with his old partner. Jerry stopped at the door and motioned him to stay. Gunter hesitated, and Jerry made a beeline to the door. When he opened it, Gunter was there, wagging his tail.

Chapter Three

Gunter stayed by Jerry's side the whole way to his cruiser, jumping inside and sitting in the passenger's seat when he opened the door.

Jerry looked at the dog and motioned to the rear of the car. "Backseat."

The dog tilted his head, pointing his long ears toward the dashboard.

"Come on. It's freaking cold out here. Get in the backseat."

Gunter answered with a single bark. Jerry sighed and slid behind the wheel. "Just so you know, I'm not a dog person. For the record, I'm not a cat person either." Jerry clicked on his seatbelt and headed out of the parking lot, leaving out the fact that he currently shared his house with an orange tabby that didn't listen any better.

Jerry thought about his promise to help find a replacement dog for Manning. He was pretty sure his friend Mike could help. The guy was prior Navy. Not that Jerry held it against the man – not everyone was cut out to be a Marine. Mike was one of the good guys. He worked with the K-9s while in the Navy and then spent years training dogs for the police department. After retiring, he began running a nonprofit that trained dogs to their highest level before donating the K-9s to police departments. He also worked to partner therapy dogs with military veterans to help them manage their PTSD. Jerry checked the time and debated calling Mike to inquire about a dog. Deciding to chance it, he made the call.

"Hello?"

"I was afraid I'd catch you in bed," Jerry replied.

"Been at it for hours. The dogs get restless if they don't get their breakfast on time. What can I do for you, Jerry?"

"I told my sergeant I'd see if you had any K-9s available." Jerry glanced over at Gunter and lowered his voice. "One of our dogs was killed in the line of duty."

"That's a damn shame. What kind of dog was he?"

"German shepherd."

"No, I mean a patrol K-9 or SAR?"

"Hell if I know. A patrol dog, I guess. The dog was trained to go on runs with the officer." Jerry covered the phone. "What kind of dog are you?"

Gunter barked his reply.

"Is that a dog I hear?"

Shit. "Yeah."

"Good. It's about time you listened to me and

got yourself a PTSD companion."

"I don't think he qualifies as a PTSD companion." Jerry slid a glance to Gunter, who'd had him on edge since the moment he'd shown up. "He doesn't listen very well."

"Has he had any training?"

Not in this lifetime. "I'm sure he's had some."

"Well, if you can get him to do the basics – sit, stay, lie down – that's a start."

"I tried to get him to get in the back seat. I think he may have laughed at me."

"That's not good, Jerry."

"Tell me about it."

"No, I mean you have to let the dog know who's in charge."

Jerry looked at the dog once more. "I'm pretty sure he knows who's in charge."

"No, that's not right. You're in charge, Jerry. You're the one who feeds him and takes him out on a leash."

"Shit."

"Shit, what? You haven't fed him or taken him out?"

Jerry realized he'd backed himself into a corner. "I guess I don't know much about dogs."

"Dogs have to eat, Jerry. How long have you had him?"

Too long. "He first showed up a couple days ago."

"A couple of days, and you haven't fed him?"

"He disappeared for a while."

"Well, he's back now, so you've got to feed him."

"I'll stop at the store on the way home."

"Not just any store; go to the pet store and get a quality dog food. Make sure the first couple of ingredients are meat. Understand? And get a good collar and a leash. What kind of dog is he?"

Jerry swallowed. "A German shepherd."

"Okay, make that a harness. And get a leash. Make sure to get a real leash, not one of those retractable ones – I don't trust those things. They snap and you're in trouble. Good choice on the dog, by the way. GSDs are good dogs, smart and very dependable. Treat him right, and he'll stay with you a long time."

"That's what I'm worried about," Jerry groaned.

"What?"

"I said I'll take care of him. You've nothing to worry about."

"So, some pointers. Don't let him on the furniture. Not until he knows you are the boss. And if he shows any sign of food aggression, feed him by hand. You need to let him know you are the provider. What's his name?"

Jerry started to say the dog's real name then stopped. The last thing he wanted was for the man to mention it to anyone. "I've just been calling him Dog."

Mike laughed. "Most dogs name themselves.

Give it some time; he'll do something that'll set him apart from all the rest."

Jerry thought to ask if being dead counted. *Maybe I should call him Casper.* "Thanks for the advice. I have to get going."

"Okay, you give your sergeant my cell number and have him give me a call. He tells me what he's looking for, and we'll find him a dog. And, Jerry?"

"Yeah, Mike?"

"You need help training that dog of yours, let me know. I've been doing this a long time. There's not a dog on this earth I can't handle."

"Okay, Mike, I'll be in touch." Jerry set the phone in the console and glanced at Gunter. "Mike said I'm supposed to show you who's boss."

Gunter curled his lip and growled a soft growl.

"Yeah, that's what I thought."

***

Never having been in a pet supply store before, Jerry wandered down the aisle marveling at all the choices. The toy aisle alone almost made him glad to have a dog. Gunter, who'd plastered himself by Jerry's side the moment they entered, stopped in front of the ball section.

"You like balls?"

Gunter gave a puppy-like yip and wagged his tail.

"Okay, a ball it is."

Jerry reached for a lime-green tennis ball, and Gunter growled. Jerry moved his hand to the right, hovering it over a smaller orange ball that reminded him of a mini basketball. Gunter yipped his approval. Jerry put the ball in the basket and continued down the aisle, stopping in front of a section of squeaky toys. He saw one that looked like an opossum, tossed it into the cart without asking the dog's approval, then continued on to the next aisle. The moment he rounded the corner, Jerry knew he was in over his head. The entire row was filled on both sides with collars, leashes, and harnesses in every color imaginable. He stopped the cart and gave a nod toward Gunter. "See anything that strikes your fancy?"

Gunter yawned his reply.

Undeterred, Jerry walked to where the harnesses were hanging, picked a red one that looked as if it would fit, then searched for a matching leash, placing them in the cart with the toys. That wasn't so bad. Now to get a bag of food and be done. The second Jerry rounded the corner to the dog food aisle, he saw a middle-aged woman with grey-streaked hair stuff a can of dog food into her coat. She had another can in her left hand, and from the bulk of the fabric, the single can of dog food wasn't the only thing hiding under the coat. She looked up as he rounded the corner and reminded him of a deer caught in the headlights. She took in his uniform, tossed the second can to the floor, then sprinted off in the opposite direction.

Before Jerry could respond, Gunter raced after the woman. Tackling her from behind, he sent her sliding along the floor a good three feet, then stood breathing down her neck, tail wagging as if it was all a glorious game.

Shit! "Dog! Get over here." Gunter did one better and disappeared.

Jerry walked to the end of the aisle and offered the woman a hand.

She slapped his hand away. "Help! Help! Police brutality!"

Several people came running, including several store employees and a man with a pit bull – both man and dog looked as if they'd never missed a meal. The dog strained against his spiked collar, and the man kept reeling in the retractable leash. Jerry thought of what Mike had said and sent out a silent prayer that the leash would hold. The man holding the leash was breathing heavy, and it was hard to tell which one was slobbering more, the man or the dog.

The man narrowed his eyes at Jerry. "You push her down?"

Jerry ignored the question, watching as the employees helped the woman to her feet.

Tears rolled from the woman's eyes. Jerry wondered if she were truly injured or afraid of getting arrested for shoplifting.

She put a hand above her heart. "I was

standing there minding my own business when that cop pushed me to the floor. I could even feel the heat of his breath on the back of my neck!"

The manager showed up before Jerry could respond. "What happened?"

"He pushed my wife!" The man with the dog let out a length of leash. "Easy, Tiny, ain't no one going to hurt your momma no more."

Jerry gave the man a closer look, wondering if the girth beneath his coat were real or if he too had been padding his beltline.

"He did. I'm going to sue. You'll hear from my attorney. All of you! I'll own this store!" She shrugged out of the employee's grip, gave her husband a nod, and they both started to walk away.

Jerry, who'd been silent up until this point, keyed his radio and requested another unit sent to his location – also specifying a female officer. Releasing the mike, he turned to the woman. "Ma'am, you need to stay where you are."

"You don't get to manhandle me and then order me around," she said over her shoulder.

"Ma'am, I'd advise you to listen. You don't want a simple case of shoplifting to turn into resisting arrest."

The woman stopped but motioned for her husband to continue.

The manager blinked his surprise. "You tackled her for shoplifting?"

"I didn't touch the woman." Jerry

maneuvered himself in front of the couple, all the while hoping the dog's leash would hold. "Sir, I suggest you stay put as well."

The man started forward once more. Jerry felt for his taser, wondering if he should use it on the man or the dog, which didn't appear happy to have Jerry so close to his human mom. Tiny growled at Jerry, barking and straining even more than before. Jerry thought back to his conversation with Mike and wondered what the man would do in his current situation. Suddenly, Jerry felt the hair on the back of his neck bristle. He held up a hand to the dog. "Easy, boy. No one's going to hurt you."

The dog's demeanor instantly changed. Cowering, he tucked his tail between his legs and began whining.

"What did you do to him?"

Jerry held up his palms. "I didn't do anything."

One of the salesmen – a young boy with the name Tim on his name tag – elbowed the other. "Check it out; the man's a real dog whisperer."

"Cesar don't have nothing on him," the other clerk agreed.

Jerry put the name of the dog and the clerk together and resisted the urge to laugh. And he wasn't a dog whisperer; he hadn't done anything except raise his hand, pretending to quiet the dog the second he felt Gunter appear. The fact that no one had mentioned the shepherd let him know they couldn't see him. While he wasn't sure if the pit bull could see Gunter, it was obvious Tiny could feel the K-9's ghostly presence. Jerry breathed a sigh of relief when he heard a local Derry Township police unit radio they'd arrived on the scene.

Jerry saw two officers enter through the sliding door. Having patrolled in the area multiple times, he recognized both Cahill and Martinez and stepped into the main aisle, positioning himself where they could see him. The door slid open a second time and admitted a third officer Jerry didn't recognize.

As the first two officers reached him, the woman pushed her way past and pointed a meaty finger at Jerry. "Thank god you're here, officers. I want you to arrest this man. I'm making a citizen's arrest, but I want you to do the arresting."

The third officer came up and quickly took charge, telling the female officer to get the woman's statement.

Jerry gave a nod to the officer, whose nametag read Barnes. "Better get one from the husband as well."

Cahill took the man and dog in the opposite direction. Though the man seemed reluctant, the dog was more than eager to leave the area.

As soon as Jerry had the man to himself, he motioned the store manager forward. "Your video cameras work?"

The manager bobbed his head. "Of course."

"Wind them back to when the couple came in. Follow them to see what the videos show. Let us know when you have it, and one of us will come take a look."

"Yes, sir, officer."

"Shoplifting," Jerry said by explanation. He looked at Gunter, who was sitting at his side looking mighty pleased with himself.

Barnes followed his gaze, appearing nonplussed. "I figured as much."

"The woman tried to run and lost her balance. She was embarrassed and blamed me for her clumsiness." Okay, it was a lie, but the video would back it up. Besides, it was better than trying to explain what really transpired.

Barnes gave a nod to the basket Jerry had left at the end of the aisle. "Is that their cart?"

"No, it's mine. I was doing a bit of shopping when I happened upon the woman feeding dog food to her coat."

Barnes looked in the cart. "Finish your shopping. I'll go have a look at the video."

While the other employee followed Barnes, Tim wavered, as if wondering if he should follow. After a few seconds of indecision, he turned his attention to Jerry. "Can I help you find something, officer?"

"Dog food."

The kid waved his hand to encompass the row of food. "What kind?"

Hell if I know. "Something with meat."

The boy laughed. "They all have meat. Some just have more than others."

Jerry looked at Gunter and shrugged. "I think the dog would like one with a lot of meat."

The boy sighed. "How big is your dog?"

Jerry held out a hand to show the height. "German shepherd."

"Okay, that helps. You're probably going to want a large breed dog food." He pointed to a bag. "This is what I feed my dog."

"You got a shepherd?"

"No, a pit. They're a wonderful breed with the right owner." He cast a glance toward the man and dog. "It was pretty cool how you got him to calm down. Your dog must be pretty well trained."

Jerry slid a glance toward Gunter, who had turned and was now staring at the boy and wagging his tail. "Son, my dog's so good, he could be right in front of you right now, and you wouldn't even know he's here."

Chapter Four

Jerry sat in the parking garage at Penn State Health Complex in Hershey, PA questioning why he was even there. To add to his distress, he'd spent the last ten minutes chiding himself for purchasing the leash and harness for the dog that seemed determined to go into the hospital with him.

I've officially lost what's left of my mind – the dog's not even real. Jerry looked at the dog, who was currently panting and dribbling droplets of saliva onto the leather seat. *Real enough to ruin the leather and to cause trouble if anyone saw him.* Though no one at the pet store could see Gunter, Holly had. Jerry wasn't sure if it was because she'd been in trouble at the time or if it was because the dog had wanted her to see him. And therein lay the problem. If some could see the dog and others could not, how would he handle the situation if confronted while walking through the hospital with an unleashed dog. And if he were actually able to put the harness and leash on the dog – without said dog biting him – what would it look like to those unable to see him?

Jerry recalled those stiff fake collared leashes of his childhood bent to look as if one were actually walking a dog. So much so, the toy companies had marketed them as invisible dogs. *I served two tours with the Marines. I'm a Pennsylvania State Trooper, and this is what my life has become. Am I really supposed to walk around pretending to walk an invisible dog? Maybe I could pretend it's a joke. No one will believe you, Jerry.*

It was all getting to be too much. Jerry looked at the dog, who sat staring at him, apparently just as confused by Jerry's indecision as Jerry himself. Jerry turned his frustration on the dog.

"Why me? You had the whole populace of earth, and you pick the one person who's not thrilled to have you here. Wouldn't you be happier with a boy who would run and play with you or, better yet, with your old partner? Sure, Manning can be a jerk, but at least he likes you."

Gunter growled, and Jerry put out his hands. "Oh no, you don't get to be angry. You're a ghost. You're not supposed to have feelings. This is all about me – I'm the one who gets to be mad."

Gunter barked a deep, throaty bark. Jerry was just about to open the door and make a run for it when he saw an older woman wearing a beige coat standing to the left of his patrol car. Leaning heavily on a cane, she had her right hand on her chest and kept turning from side to side.

Jerry set the leash and harness aside and got out of the car. "Can I help you, ma'am?"

"Oh, I don't want to be a bother. It's just that I can't seem to find my car. I thought for sure I'd parked on this level. I was almost certain of it. But it's not here."

Jerry looked at Gunter, who'd followed him out of the car. "We'll help you find it."

The woman looked from Jerry to the car and back to Jerry again. "We?"

Shit. "You and me together. Do you have your car keys?"

"My keys aren't going to do me any good if I can't find my car."

"Ah, but they will." At least he hoped so. "Dig them out, and I'll show you a trick."

She unzipped her purse and dug around inside before finally retrieving a set of keys and handing them over with trembling hands. "I still don't know what good they'll do without the car."

Jerry held them up then pressed the lock button. Though he couldn't hear anything, Gunter barked then took off running. Jerry thought about following then changed his mind. "I think you are on a different level."

She looked uncertain. "How can you be so sure. I thought for sure I'd parked on this level. Perhaps someone stole it. Maybe you should call it in on that there radio of yours."

"How about we check the garage first? If we

don't find your car, I promise to call it in." He took her by the elbow. "Come on, and I'll give you a ride."

Her blue eyes twinkled. "I've never ridden in a police car before."

Jerry led her to the passenger side and started to open the front door, when she stopped him.

"Could I maybe ride in the back seat?"

Jerry suppressed a chuckle. "Sure."

She retrieved her cell phone from her right coat pocket and held it out to him. "And could you maybe take a picture of me to prove it?"

Jerry thought to ask if she wanted him to handcuff her but decided against it. She grinned a wide grin while he took several photos. He started to hand the phone back, then hesitated. "You know, most criminals are not smiling when they are sitting back there."

"Oh…Oh." She rifled her hand through her hair and scrunched her face into a frown. "How's this?"

Jerry snapped a couple more photos and handed her the phone so she could see for herself.

The woman snickered her approval and placed the phone back in her pocket. "Just wait until I post these on the Facebook. My friends at the bingo hall are going to be so jealous."

Shit. Way to go, Jerry. Why don't you cruise around with lights and sirens blaring for good measure? He shut the door, walked to the driver's side of the cruiser, and got in. He pulled out of the space and watched in his rearview mirror as someone claimed the spot that had taken three full turns around the parking garage to find. He circled to the next floor and onto the next before seeing Gunter standing in front of a blue PT Cruiser. He pulled up next to the car and looked in the mirror once more. "Would that be yours?"

She looked out the window and gasped her surprise. "Why, yes, it is. How did you know?"

"It matches your eyes." *Jesus, Jerry.*

"That's exactly what my husband said when he bought it for me."

Jerry placed the cruiser in park and walked around, opening the door for her. As he helped her from his car, he pointed to the concrete pillar. "Next time you come, use your cell phone to take a photo of the sign. When you're finished with your appointment, you can check the picture to see where you parked your car."

"What a smart young man you are."

"And don't put your keys in your purse. Keep them in your pocket, so you don't have to dig for them in case anyone is following you."

"That's a good idea. People are always following me when I'm in here."

Jerry raised an eyebrow. "They are?"

"Oh yes, it's the only way to get a parking place. Speaking of which, you'd better take mine when I leave. You're not likely to get your old spot back."

Jerry helped her to her car, declined the tip she offered, then backed up and waited for her to pull out so he could snag her parking spot. He turned to Gunter, who'd returned to the passenger seat. "You should go home with her. She seems nice enough."

Gunter growled his answer.

"What? At least if she forgets you in the car, you'll be able to get out on your own." Jerry held up the harness, moved to place it over Gunter's head, then made a mental note to return it to the store when the dog bared his teeth. "Okay, but I'll deny knowing you if anyone sees you."

Jerry's cell rang, the ringtone letting him know it was Sergeant Seltzer. "Hey, Sarge, what's up?"

"Just letting you know I got a call from Derry Township."

"They reviewed the video while I was still in the store. I never touched the woman."

"Never said you did."

"So why'd they call?"

"When the woman threatened to sue, the watch captain decided to review the videos a second time. Though he agreed you were nowhere near the woman, he questioned your overall behavior. He seems to think you were acting a bit odd in the store."

"How so?"

"He claims you were talking to yourself. I told him there must be a reasonable explanation for your actions."

"In other words, you lied." Or *covered my ass, again.*

"I give all my officers the benefit of the doubt until I see the evidence."

Jerry closed his eyes and let out a sigh. Even before the dog came into the picture, he knew his days at the post to be numbered. Still, he'd thought he had a bit more time to figure things out. "What do you think?"

"I try not to when it comes to you."

Jerry cast a glance toward the dog. "When are you going to review the clip?"

"The store manager's waiting for approval from his boss. Then he'll e-mail it over."

"So why tell me. Why not just hit me with it when I come in?"

"What, and deprive you of a chance to come up with a plausible explanation?"

"Maybe I should just tell the truth."

"Would it get you kicked off the force?"

Jerry looked at the dog once more. "Probably."

Seltzer sighed into the phone. "Work on your story, McNeal. We'll talk tomorrow."

Jerry clicked off the phone and stuck it into his pocket. *Tomorrow it is.*

***

Gunter stayed with Jerry the entire way to the visitor information station. Several hospital volunteers sat behind the desk. One looked up when he approached. Gunter jumped up, placing his paws on the counter directly in front of the woman. Jerry smiled a disarming smile and asked for Holly's room number. The woman looked him over and frowned.

Shit, she sees the dog. Jerry decided to face the dilemma head-on. "Is there a problem?"

"What? No, I was about to ask you the same thing, officer."

The uniform. Jerry felt his tension ease. "Not at all. Just here visiting a friend."

"Oh, good." She wrote Holly's room number on a map of the complex and handed it to him. As she slid the paper over, Gunter licked the back of the woman's age-spotted hand. Though she didn't acknowledge the dog's gesture, she covered the spot with her other hand when she pulled it away. She smiled a confused smile. "You have a good day, officer."

Why is it everyone else gets tail wags and licks, and all I get are growls? For the first time, Jerry realized the dog's rejection actually bothered him. Why had Gunter attached himself to him when it was apparent from his actions that the dog didn't even like him? Jerry pondered that question the whole way through the maze of hallways and onto the elevator. He was still questioning things when he approached Holly's room. The door to the room was open, but the curtain was pulled so that Jerry could not see inside. He started to knock then hesitated when

Gunter moved between him and the door. Frustrated, Jerry began to reach over the dog.

Gunter growled his objection.

This is getting ridiculous. Jerry was about to say something about calling an exorcist, when he heard Holly's voice.

"I can't do this anymore, Dad. It's not fair to Gracie."

"You're overreacting. Gracie is doing much better."

"I know she's better, and that's precisely the point. If I'm going to make the move, I need to do it now. Get her settled into a new life and established with doctors now while she is healthy."

"But why move at all?"

"Because she needs to be around family. If this had been worse…"

"It wasn't."

"But it almost was, Dad. Then what would have happened to her?"

"I would have taken care of her."

"Dad, you know I love you, but you can barely take care of yourself."

"Who will take care of me if you're not here?"

There was a moment of silence. "I was hoping you would come with us."

"I don't know."

"They are your family too. It just makes sense. Gracie needs to know her extended family. That way, if anything happens to us, she won't be thrust into a sea of strangers. She has aunts and uncles that she's only seen a handful of times. Please, Dad. Aunt Edna said we can stay with her until we find a place of our own."

"What about that nice young man you were telling me about? I thought you said there was a connection."

"You mean the one I haven't heard from since the accident? He's a cop, Dad. He was only doing his job."

No, I'm here. Jerry tried to step around the dog, hoping to let Holly know she was wrong. Gunter bared his teeth, once again refusing to allow him to enter the room.

"I don't need any distractions, Dad. I need stability."

"You both need someone dependable in your life."

"We do, which is why I'm hoping you'll move with us. I can't imagine not having you close, but in the end, I need to do what is best for my daughter."

"Okay, Holly. I'll go with you."

Jerry turned away from the room and retraced his steps to the elevator. As he stood waiting for the doors to open, he looked at Gunter, who was now staring up at him with soft brown eyes. If not for the K-9, he would've gone into the room and possibly changed the direction of Holly's life. The woman needed dependable, and that wasn't him. It had never been him. At the moment, it was unclear if he'd even have a job much longer.

"Is this it? Is this why you're here? To keep me from ruining her life?" As if in answer to Jerry's question, Gunter wagged his tail. A second later, the dog disappeared.

Chapter Five

Jerry woke with the feeling of being watched. He opened his eyes, expecting to see the cat staring at him, but Cat was nowhere in sight. Odd, as it was well past his normal feeding time.

Jerry sat on the edge of the bed, doing his best to shake his unease. He showered, then dressed and made his way to the kitchen. The feeling intensified as he poured himself a cup of coffee and took a sip, lingering as he placed the cup on the table. *What's going on, Jerry?*

Jerry made a show of getting out the can of cat food, opening the container, and putting it on the floor with a clang. Cat was not one for missing a meal, and Jerry was surprised he wasn't already rubbing against his leg, purring in excited anticipation.

"Yo, Cat, breakfast is ready." *Where the hell are you?* Jerry retrieved his cup and walked through the house, searching his usual hangouts. By the time he'd walked through the whole place, Jerry had to admit feeling concerned, wondering if he had accidentally left him outside. Just as he was about to give up, he caught sight of the cat out of the corner of his eye. Ears plastered back and eyes wide, Cat sat on top of the refrigerator watching his every move.

"How the hell did you get up there?" Jerry walked over to help him down, surprised when Cat hissed at him. Another attempt had the cat emitting a low warning growl. What the heck was it with animals growling at him?

Jerry withdrew his hand. "What the hell has gotten into you, Cat? It was your idea to stay. You don't like it here, you're welcome to leave. If I'd wanted a cat, I would've given you a name other than Cat. I remember distinctly warning you that I don't even like cats."

Jerry's comment evoked another low growl.

"Geesh, Cat, you got rabies or something?" Jerry asked, only half-joking. His brain told him the stray had been here so long that rabies would have presented itself by now, but something sure had the animal on edge. It reminded him of a person dealing with PTSD – that was one ailment Jerry was well-versed in.

He walked across the room, picked up the can of cat food, and brought it back to the cat. Cat sniffed the contents and took a bite. As he ate, he continued to grumble his discontent.

"Cat, I don't mind if you eat up there, but you'd better not use the area as a litterbox. That shit will get your ass booted out for sure."

Jerry moved to the window and stood drinking his coffee. Even though his head and neck were freshly shaven, he felt tingling on the back of his neck where the hair should be, crawling like a zillion bugs up and down his neck and across his arms as he stared off into the distance.

As he took another sip from his cup, he saw something move. Looking closer, Jerry realized what he saw was not outside the window but a reflection of something moving behind him. The practical part of his brain told him Cat had finally evacuated his hiding place, but the part of his brain that looked elsewhere warned him this was not the case. Palming the cup in case he needed to use it as a weapon, he turned from the window. His breath caught, and his grip tightened around the cup, even though he knew it would prove ineffective against the current threat.

In the center of the floor, crouched but alert, Gunter stared back at him – eyes so intense that Jerry could barely breathe. So much for his theory that the dog had come to keep him from ruining Holly's life. Also now debunked was Jerry's original theory that the K-9's appearance was limited to police activities. His presence in the apartment seemed to have Gunter confused as well – the ghostly apparition stared at him as if it were Jerry who was out of place.

Cat hissed, drawing Jerry's attention.

"Yeah, I see him too. The bad news, he's a ghost. The good news, I don't think he can actually eat either one of us."

The dog barked, making Jerry question his earlier deduction. Cat crouched down, pressing himself further against the back wall above the fridge. For a brief second, Jerry considered joining him.

Take it easy, Jerry. If the dog were going to eat you, he would have done so already. He was fine – well, mostly fine – in the car yesterday. Something must be upsetting him. Or maybe it's just because he doesn't like unfamiliar settings. Then again, he's a police dog. He's been trained to handle the unknown. Does training transfer over to the other realm? Think of Cujo. Cujo wasn't dead; he had rabies. Okay, what about the cat from Pet Cemetery? What was his name? Before he could recall the cat's name, the dog growled a throaty growl. *Do something, Jerry. What was it Manning used to say to him?*

"At ease, Dog," Jerry commanded.

The dog barked his answer.

"At ease, Gunter!" Jerry firmed the command and called the dog by name. It was a long shot, but he'd heard Manning give the dog the same command on multiple occasions to call the dog off.

Instantly, the dog's demeanor changed. No longer on alert, the dog crouched, wagging his tail. Jerry rolled his shoulders. *Okay, that's more like it.*

"You want some grub, dog?" Jerry walked to the fridge, pulled out a slice of ham, and tossed it in front of the dog.

The dog sniffed it but made no move to eat.

"Go on, dog, take it."

Nothing.

"Eat, Gunter." Still nothing. Jerry shook his head and took another sip of coffee. "Why me, Lord? First, I have a cat I didn't ask for, and now I'm being haunted by Cujo."

The dog growled. A second later, there was a knock on the front door. Jerry glanced at the door. When he looked back, the dog was gone. Also missing was the feeling that had been hanging in the air before he appeared.

Jerry crossed the living space of the small upstairs apartment he rented and opened the door to find his landlord, Todd Wells, standing on the landing, shivering and blowing into his ungloved hands. Wells appeared agitated, and Jerry braced himself for another tirade from the man who'd been onto Jerry for the last couple of weeks, asking if he was going to renew his lease. Jerry had signed the original lease, three years with an option for three more, to coincide with his patrol rotation. While he'd initially intended to stay, recently, something was telling Jerry to hold off. Though he didn't know the reason, Jerry knew better than to question his feelings – especially one so strong.

The thing was, Jerry had spent the better part of the previous year making improvements to the place. The agreement was that Jerry would do the renovations, and Wells would deduct the materials from the price of rent. Jerry had thought it a good deal at the time, as the man had given him the go-ahead to pick the finishes, meaning Jerry was able to get the look he wanted without shelling out the dough for a high-end apartment. Wells hadn't objected, as the deal assured him free labor. Both had been happy with the agreement until the renovations were completed – Wells took one look at the newly updated garage apartment and saw dollar signs. From that moment, he'd tried every underhanded trick available to convince Jerry not to renew his lease.

Jerry was not stupid. If Wells could force him out, he could ask three times the price Jerry currently paid for the formerly outdated unit. While Jerry liked the place, he wasn't sure if he liked it enough to deal with Wells' crap for the next three years. But that didn't mean he intended to give his landlord the satisfaction of leaving early. The contract was not due to expire for two months, and he was only required to provide a thirty-day notice.

Jerry stared at the man, wondering what new thing he'd invented to needle him about today.

"Mr. McNeal, do you think carrying a badge gives you the right to break the law?" Jerry blinked his confusion as Wells stood on his tippy toes and tried to look around him. It wasn't the first time the man had tried this tactic.

"What law would I be breaking this time?"

"I heard a dog." Wells held up what looked to be his copy of the contract. "Our agreement specifically states no pets, and I heard a dog. Erma heard it too."

Shit! "Mr. Wells, I assure you I don't own a dog." Technically, it was the truth.

Wells was not convinced. "McNeal, it's bad enough you're standing there lying to me, but Erma heard it too. Shame on you, and you being a police officer and all."

Erma was Well's hundred-plus-pound Old English bulldog who did nothing but eat, bark, and shit all over the yard. It was disgusting enough dodging the piles in the summertime, but he despised looking at them in the winter. Dark cigar-length blemishes marring all the fresh white snow. While dogs had never liked Jerry, his disdain for dogs took on a whole new level after meeting Erma – not that it was the dog's fault. Jerry didn't want a dog. Any dog. The last thing he wanted was to run after some mutt and pick up shit all day.

Jerry pulled himself to attention and raised his voice just in case the dog had any plans to make itself visible to the man at the door. "I'm a Pennsylvania State Trooper. I do not own nor do I wish to have a dog!"

"Well, you don't have to yell," Wells admonished. "Just let me come in and have a look around, and that will be the end of it."

Wells attempted to enter, and Jerry blocked his way. "Do you have a search warrant?"

"I don't need a blasted search warrant to enter my own property."

"No, but you do need to give me twenty-four hours' notice according to that lease in your hand."

"What about probable cause?"

"That only works for the police," Jerry reminded him.

"What if I call the police? They would have to come, right?"

Jerry chuckled. "The police would come, eventually. Then they would take your statement. Next, they would come up here and ask me if I have a dog."

"And you would lie to them, just like you're lying to me right now."

"I would tell them the truth. The same as I already told you."

"And they would believe you because you have a badge."

Jerry sighed. "Because I'm telling the truth."

Wells cupped his hands and blew air into them.

"You're cold, Mr. Wells. Go home and come back tomorrow."

Wells cocked his head.

"You've asked to see inside. Come back tomorrow at this time, and I'll let you in."

"You trying to be cute?"

"No, sir, just trying to uphold the law. You asked to see inside. I'll let you in when the required twenty-four-hour notice is up."

"I see what you're doing. It will give you time to tamper with the evidence."

Jerry resisted the urge to push the man down the stairs. "Go home, Wells."

"And if I refuse?"

"Then I'll help you down the stairs. I'm sure they are mighty slippery with all this new snow. It'd be too bad if you were to happen to fall down a couple on the way down."

Wells narrowed his eyes. "That would be police brutality."

"I'm not in uniform. Besides, I have a darn good lawyer. I'm pretty sure we can get you on faulty upkeep of the premises. Might even be able to call in the sewer commissioner to give you a fine for not picking up after your dog. I'm fairly certain there is an ordinance about feces going into the storm drains. While I'm at it, I will insist they call PETA because I'm pretty sure that hound of yours is grossly overweight." Jerry was reaching for stuff, but from the look on Wells' face, the man was buying into it.

"I'll be back in the morning. And you can believe I will be watching you. You try to sneak a dog out of here, and I'll know it."

Not if the dog is invisible. Jerry closed the door. The second he did, the dog reappeared.

Chapter Six

Weary from the long drive from Louisville, Savannah pulled into her sister's driveway in Chambersburg, Pennsylvania, happy to have finally reached her destination. She grabbed her phone to text her sister of her arrival, when the speakers in the car's dashboard alerted her of her sister's call. Savannah pressed the button on the display. "Reading my mind again?"

"I'd love to say yes, but I got an alert on my phone telling me someone was in the driveway."

"You're not home?"

"No, I just got off work. My car is still in the shop. It was supposed to be finished this morning, but now they're saying Monday. Anyway, I rode in with a friend last night. Want to pick me up? He doesn't get off for another hour."

Savannah stared at the dashboard. "He?"

"Just a co-worker. You going to pick me up or not?"

"Sure, but I'm going to need a nap when we get back here."

"No time for that. We've got to set things up before everyone arrives."

Savannah sighed. "Ugh, I tossed and turned until two and finally said the heck with it and got on the road. The weather in the mountains was awful, and I'm beat."

"Yeah, well, I worked a double, so we get to be miserable together."

"I'm going to need a huge amount of caffeine to make it through the day."

"You and me both. Straight up Lincoln Highway and follow the signs to the hospital, remember?"

"I remember."

"Just come to the Emergency entrance. I'll keep an eye out for you."

Savannah put her car in reverse and drove the short distance, stifling a yawn as she made the right onto Lincoln Highway. She cruised through several traffic lights before finally getting caught by a red. There was a combination gas station convenience store on the right, so she clicked on her turn signal, thinking to pick up a coffee. The light changed just as she began to turn the wheel, and she reconsidered, deciding she was too tired to get out of the car. A few short blocks later, she saw the sign to the hospital, turned right onto North 7th Street, then made a right and navigated into the Emergency bay. Still dressed in scrubs, Cassidy stood just inside the door. She hurried to the car and immediately started fiddling with the heater.

Savannah batted her hand away. "If you're

cold, zip your coat. It took me two hundred miles, but I finally had it adjusted to where I wanted it."

Cassidy looked her over. "You look like hell."

Savannah let off of the brake and eased out from underneath the overhang. "You don't look so hot yourself. Are those bags under your eyes?"

Her sister shrugged. "Nothing a bit of makeup won't hide. Take a right."

"Aren't we going back to Lincoln Highway?"

"Yes, but you can't make a left from this street. Go right, take your first left, then it will take you around where you can turn left at the light."

Savannah turned the wheel and followed her sister's instructions. "Why'd you work a double if you knew you'd be hosting the convention tonight?"

"A friend's kid got sick, and she didn't have anyone to watch her." She pointed, motioning for Savannah to make a turn. "It's all good. She covered for me a few weeks ago."

"That's sweet of you, Cass."

"I know. And it's Raven."

"What is?"

"My name."

"When did that happen?"

"Today. It goes better with my outfit. I've got one for you too."

"I like my name."

"That's because you like the history that surrounds it."

It was true. Their mother used to regale the girls with stories of why she'd chosen their names. Savannah was named after the city where their parents had spent their honeymoon. Cassidy, on the other hand, was named after the band their mother was listening to the first time her parents had done the deed. Why their mother couldn't have simply told Cassidy she'd been named after Mama Cass and been done with it remained a mystery.

"Because Mom took pleasure in torturing me."

"Stop reading my mind."

Cassidy laughed. "I didn't have to; your mind always goes there when we talk about how we got our names."

"It's hard not to go there. Mom shared the story enough over the years."

"Which is why she's going to stay with you when she gets old and senile. It's bad enough listening to the story while she has all her faculties. I refuse to do so when I can't tell her to knock it off."

"I don't think we have to worry about her losing her mind anytime soon. Her memory is better than mine."

"That's good. Hey, I got you an outfit to show off the ladies."

Savannah slid a glance in her sister's direction, knowing the comment to be a thinly veiled dig at their mother, who, in Cassidy's mind, had purposely saved the breast gene for Savannah. She'd heard it many times over the years, *Mom likes you best; she gave you a better name and better breasts.* It wasn't that Savannah minded showing off her breasts, but not having much to show for herself, she felt that Cassidy sometimes pushed things to the extreme. "Still trying to dress me like a slut?"

"We've been through this before. You'll probably be the youngest reader in the room. That's not a bad thing, but people might see your youth as a sign of inexperience. I've seen it before; people gravitate to the older psychics because they think they're wiser."

Savannah held up her left hand to show her newly acquired wedding ring. "I'm old enough to be married."

Cassidy ignored both the ring and comment. "You're still young. If you want to stand out, you have to let the ladies breathe."

"So I can draw in the creeps." Savannah pulled into the convenience store she'd almost stopped at on her way to pick up her sister. "I need caffeine."

Cassidy unbuckled her seatbelt and turned to face her. "It's not like you're leaving with any of them. I'll put you in the front row so I can keep an eye on you. We'll work out a signal, then if you need me to save you, I will. Listen, it won't always be like this. You have the gift; I've seen it firsthand. Being at the convention will help you gain confidence."

Cassidy had a point. While she had no trouble picking up on things, she lacked the experience to give a proper reading, especially if the message she received was one the person sitting across from her wouldn't enjoy hearing. As much as she enjoyed her ability, she despised being the bearer of bad news. Her sister, on the other hand, was extremely adept at handling every situation thrown at her. "Okay, I'll listen to your advice."

Cassidy opened the door. "You coming in?"

"No, I'm saving my energy for tonight. Forget the coffee, get me a monster drink – the more caffeine the better. Don't look now, but the cops are here." Savannah nodded to the state cruiser, which had pulled in and was currently backing into a parking space near the road.

Cassidy shrugged off the comment. "They're always here. The state police post is not too far away."

The moment her sister shut the door, Savannah readjusted the heat. She looked through the store window, wishing she'd told Cassidy to bring her a donut. Smiling, she closed her eyes, pictured her sister's face, and conjured up the image of a chocolate donut with multicolored sprinkles. As she concentrated, she felt someone watching her. She opened her eyes, half expecting to see Cassidy staring out the window sticking out her tongue. She wasn't there, but the feeling of being watched intensified. She scanned the parking lot, a chill racing down her spine when her gaze came to rest on the police cruiser. Though the officer had gone inside, the car was idling – white smoke drifting out from the tailpipe.

She wiped the fog from her window, surprised to see a large German shepherd staring back at her from the patrol car's passenger seat. Strange that he was watching her and not the door that his owner had used. It also struck her odd that the dog was sitting in the front seat, as she'd always thought them confined to the back. The intensity of the dog's stare pulled at her, that and the fact that she'd always been fascinated with German shepherds.

Hoping to get a better look, she put her car in reverse and drove past the cop car. The dog locked eyes on her, watching her as she passed. Brown with black markings, the dog's ears pointed straight to the roof of the car. Well, one of them did. The other seemed to have a piece missing. Even with the defect, it was a stunning dog. A car came up behind her, and she moved forward, then turned around, driving slowly to get another look. She lowered the side window and whistled – smiling when the dog tilted its head in response.

A horn blared. Savannah looked in her rearview mirror and saw a red truck pressed close to the back of her car. When she looked back at the police car, the dog was gone. She circled around the pumps and reached the door just as her sister exited the store.

Cassidy opened the passenger door, got in, and immediately adjusted the thermostat. "Now this is what I call service. I got you your donut; sorry, they were all out of sprinkles."

"I can't believe it still works."

Cassidy pulled a chocolate donut from the bag and handed it to her. "Always has."

Savannah drove past the police car on the way out of the back parking lot. "I wanted to get a better look at the police dog. He must have lay down."

"I should have known. You've always been drawn to animals." Cassidy pulled the top on the can and handed it to her. "Maybe that's the direction you should go."

"A K-9 officer?"

"God, no. You'd shoot someone. But there's big money in pet psychics."

"Seriously?" She loved working with animals and wouldn't mind getting paid for it.

"Sure. The pet business is a billion-dollar industry. It's something to think about."

"Does that mean I don't have to wear the dress?"

Cassidy laughed. "Oh, you're going to wear

the dress. You might even meet yourself a nice guy."

So her sister hadn't missed the comment about being married. It wouldn't surprise her if she'd been dwelling on it the whole time. It was no secret that Cassidy disapproved of her relationship with Alex – enough so that she had even made excuses for not being able to take time off from work to drive to Kentucky to attend the private ceremony. "Somehow, I doubt Alex would like that."

"Ah yes, Alex. How is married life treating you?"

"I couldn't be happier." Hoping to avoid another fight over the fact that Cassidy hadn't so much as sent a card, Savannah changed the subject. "There was something about the dog. No, I think there's more to it than that. The moment I saw the car – even before I saw the dog – I got chills."

"I felt it too."

"With the cop car?"

"No, the cop. I saw him inside. He felt it too. I could tell."

"Really? Did he say anything?"

"No, but it was there. Something in the way he looked at me."

The light turned green, and Savannah moved forward with the traffic. "Maybe he has a thing for nurses."

"Perhaps. Though he'd have to be desperate

to find me attractive today."

"That's true."

"Hey!"

"You're wearing scrubs and a pink puff coat. Your hair is in a bun, and you look as if you haven't slept in a week."

"I hate to break it to you, but you don't look much better."

Savannah checked the mirror and sighed. "We're going to need a lot of makeup!"

Cassidy held up a bag with several cans of caffeinated beverages. "And a lot more caffeine."

Chapter Seven

Jerry knew something was wrong when he stepped inside the station, and everyone turned in his direction. Instead of the usual *hey, Jerry, what's happening*, his fellow officers now stared at him much the way one stared at a criminal that had perpetrated a particularly heinous crime. Manning stepped out from behind his cubicle, made eye contact, then looked past Jerry as if looking for someone – or something.

It occurred to Jerry that Gunter might have taken this moment to reveal himself to the unit and resisted looking over his shoulder. What if he had? Should he feign shock? Would it matter? They already thought him to be a bit off – not that he cared what any of them thought. Only he did. They were a great bunch of guys. Outstanding officers that had treated him like just one of the guys – until he proved them wrong. It had been that way throughout his life – which was why he was more comfortable on his own.

Perhaps it wasn't the dog at all; maybe in his bid to reclaim some semblance of order between Cat and the dog, he'd somehow forgotten to put on pants. No, he specifically remembered changing into his uniform pants after Wells left. *Don't try to kid yourself, Jerry; you know good and well what Manning's looking for – he damn sure isn't trying to figure out if you're wearing boxers or briefs. The dog.* He wasn't sure how they'd found out, but it was pretty obvious they had. It was the only explanation for his fellow officers standing there looking at him as if he had the plague.

Ignoring their stares, Jerry walked to his cubicle, placed his hat in the chair, and continued to the coffee station, taking his time to fill his cup. *Just act normal, Jerry. What a joke; there's nothing normal about you. Never has been and never will be.*

Most of the time, he didn't give a rat's ass what anyone else thought, but ever since the dog had shown up, even he had questioned his sanity. *Come on, Jerry, stop being so dramatic – it's not like you haven't seen ghosts before.*

Jerry wondered what Seltzer thought of the situation. It wasn't like he hadn't tried to warn the man. *Yeah, and then you passed it off as a joke the second he acted as if he didn't believe you. You should have tried harder.* The fact that his sergeant hadn't already made an appearance spoke for itself. It was clear the man had finally reached his limit. Unable to delay any longer, Jerry went to Seltzer's office.

The door was open. Seltzer looked up and

motioned him in. "Kick the door around, McNeal."

Jerry shut the door and stood rigid in front of his desk.

Seltzer waved him off. "At ease, McNeal. You're not on report."

Jerry relaxed but continued to stand.

Seltzer got up and looked around the room before walking to the window and looking out. "The video came in from Hershey. I'm not the only one who saw it. Peters saw it as well. He's worked a few cases with them, so I'm guessing they already had his e-mail plugged in. Still, he didn't have to show it to the others."

"I didn't push the woman."

"That part was obvious."

"I get the feeling there's a but in there."

"What the hell were you doing in the store?"

"Shopping."

"For a dog you don't own and talking to a person that wasn't there," Seltzer blurted.

So that was it. The guys didn't know about his ghostly visitor. They just thought he was crazy. Jerry pondered his new dilemma. Was one level of crazy better than the other? Would either option allow him to remain on the job? Did he even want to stay? Too many questions and not enough answers. He needed some time to work out his response. "Can I see the evidence?"

Seltzer hesitated briefly, then shrugged. "You're going to see it eventually. Might as well have a look."

Jerry waited for Seltzer to pull up the video, watching the set of the man's mouth as he turned the screen around. It must be bad if the sergeant couldn't find a reason to make a quip. The video clip began with Jerry walking into the store. Uniform pressed and brimmed hat sitting high upon his sleek head, Jerry walked through the sliding door like a man on a mission. Though Jerry knew Gunter to have been at his side, the dog wasn't present in the video. *Then why had he shown up in the photo Holly took?* Just thinking of Holly pulled at his heart.

Focus, Jerry.

Jerry blinked and refocused his attention on the video, which showed him starting up the aisle that held the dog toys. He stopped pushing the cart and appeared to be speaking to someone. He was getting ready to tell his boss that he'd been singing along with the music when the video showed him reaching for a ball. He questioned the invisible entity then chose another. The evidence showed him doing something similar twice more before leaving the aisle. By the time he'd watched the entire clip, even Jerry further questioned his mental stability.

Seltzer canceled the file then pulled up another one that started with Jerry coming face to face with his accuser. The woman bolted the second she saw him – running away on her own accord. A second before she fell, Jerry lifted a hand and splayed his fingers – mouthing something that sent her sliding across the floor. *Shit*.

"There's another clip if you want to see it. It zooms in on your mouth and clearly shows you telling the woman to stop."

"Would you have preferred me to shoot her for shoplifting?"

Seltzer eyeballed him before replaying the last scene. He stopped at the point where Jerry lifted his hand. "I watched this a dozen times. The more I view it, the more I feel like I'm watching a movie where the sorcerer casts a spell on someone. A few special effects and you've got yourself a viral Tik-Tok video. Seriously, McNeal, I don't know what to tell Derry, much less the guys in the department."

Jerry wasn't worried about Derry. After telling the woman they had video of her and her husband shoplifting, both had admitted to their crimes. "Hershey isn't a problem."

"And the men in the other room?"

No guts, no glory, Jerry. "Tell them the truth."

Seltzer raised an eyebrow. "How about you start by telling me?"

"I did. Or at least I tried to. Right here in this room yesterday."

Seltzer stared at Jerry, mouth agape. "The dog?"

"Yep."

Seltzer pulled a stick of gum from a pack, unwrapped it, and stuck it in his mouth, then offered one to Jerry, who declined. "You mean to tell me that Gunter has returned from the dead?"

"Yep."

"And it was the dog that pushed the woman down?"

"It's the truth. Listen, I know that I can feel things before they happen and see things that aren't there, but that's where my abilities stop." Jerry held out his hands, turning them to show they were simply hands. "If you want to call those things magic, so be it. But I assure you that is where my 'gift' ends. I'm not a sorcerer, warlock, or any of the other things your mind might conjure up."

Seltzer blew out a whistle. "So you're telling me the dog did it?"

Jerry nodded.

"I always thought of ghosts as a mist of some sort. I didn't know they could be firm enough to send a person flying like that."

Jerry was genuinely surprised his sergeant admitted to having given ghosts any thought at all. "Not every accident is as innocent as it seems. Have you ever tripped over your own two feet, stumbled up the stairs, or caught your finger in a car door?"

Seltzer's eyes grew wide. "Jesus, McNeal, we have a hard enough time trying to prosecute the living. You can't go around telling people stuff like that."

"I don't intend to."

Seltzer stopped chewing his gum. "You want me to tell them?"

Jerry shook his head. "Those guys aren't going to believe either of us."

"I'm not following you, McNeal."

"We just need to convince one."

Seltzer leaned back in his chair. "If we convince Manning, he does the rest."

Jerry nodded.

"Any idea how you intend on getting the man to believe you?"

"Not a clue."

Seltzer smiled. "Glad to hear you have things under control. When do you want to do this?"

"I guess now's as good a time as any."

"You mean the dog's here?"

"Appeared a few minutes after I came into the room."

Seltzer stood, peered over the desk, and sighed his disappointment. "McNeal, if I didn't know better, I would swear you're pulling my leg."

"I wouldn't do that, sir."

"I know, which is the only reason I haven't requested your gun and badge. What now?"

"Call Manning in and pray something comes to me."

Seltzer lifted his phone, punched in the

numbers to Manning's desk, telling him to come to his office, then lowered the receiver. "I hope this works."

"You and me both."

Gunter jumped up, placing his paws on Seltzer's desk, and barked at the monitor. Not only did Jerry know what the dog was trying to convey, but he thought it was a splendid idea. "Did Derry send you the whole video?"

"They did, but I haven't looked at it all." He smiled a sheepish grin. "I kind of lost my stomach for it after I saw you cast the spell."

"Understood. While I'm talking to Manning, pull it up. Pause it when you see me first get to the toy aisle." Jerry felt Manning's presence even before the man cleared his throat to announce his appearance.

"You wanted to see me, sir?"

Seltzer motioned him in and pointed at the chair next to Jerry. Manning pulled the chair to the side and sat leaning far away from Jerry.

Jerry gripped the sidearms of his chair, thinking to slide his chair closer. Seltzer shot him a look that said *you wanted this meeting*, and Jerry thought better of it. Staying where he was, he turned his body toward Manning. "There's no easy way to say this, so I'll just say it and be done. Gunter's ghost is here, and he seems to have taken an interest in me."

Manning fist-pumped the air, grinning like a boy who'd just gotten his first kiss. "I knew it!"

No way it could be that easy. Jerry looked at Seltzer, who also blinked his disbelief, then turned back to Manning. "You're not surprised?"

"No offense, McNeal, but when it comes to you, nothing surprises me."

"None taken. So you're saying you've seen him?"

"No, just a feeling. Not like your feelings," Manning added a little too quickly. "But ever since our little run-in yesterday, I've gotten the feeling I wasn't alone. Not all the time, but enough to know something was up."

"Do you feel him now?"

Manning nodded his head and looked beside his chair. The problem was that the dog was nowhere near where the man was looking.

Jerry did a head tilt to let Seltzer know the situation. Great, either the man was trying to humor him or was still grieving so much he wanted to feel the dog's presence. Jerry decided to go with the latter. "I think he thinks he's still alive. He's still on the job and has helped me twice."

Manning bristled. "Why's he helping you? I'm his partner."

"Maybe it's because I can see him."

Manning's face turned red, and he pulled back the hand that had been pretending to pet the dog. "You can?"

"When he wants me to. He was just at your side."

69

Manning looked at the spot beside the chair, and Jerry looked at Seltzer, who'd obviously caught the lie. "You got that video, Sergeant?"

"I do." Seltzer turned the screen around.

Jerry pointed to the monitor. "You've seen the video, right?"

Manning nodded. "I have."

"Go ahead and push play."

Seltzer did, and Jerry pointed to the screen once more. "Gunter was with me in the store. Walking on my left side."

"He always walked on my left." Manning sighed a heavy sigh. "I wish I could see him."

"You will. In just a minute." Seltzer started to object, and Jerry raised a hand to silence him. The video showed Jerry reaching for a ball. "Stop the video. I started to pick out a ball, and Gunter stopped me because he didn't like the ball. Start the video."

Manning gasped when Jerry moved his hand to a different ball. "That kind was always his favorite. He never liked tennis balls, only the rubber ones."

The video showed Jerry coming face to face with the woman and showed her dropping the can. She took off running, then crashed to the floor. Manning jumped up and bit at the back of his knuckle while pointing at the screen with his other hand. "Oh man, I could see him running and slamming into her. Not on the video, but I've seen Gunter do it enough that I could tell what happened."

Sergeant Seltzer started to stop the video, and Jerry shook his head. "Let it run."

Seltzer moved to see the screen better, and they all watched as the manager and several employees came into view. A man joined them, struggling to maintain control of an obese pit bull that seemed to have taken exception to Jerry.

"His name's Tiny." Jerry motioned to the screen. "Gunter is about to take control of the scene. He'd disappeared after the manager showed up but came back just as I thought the leash would break. The instant I felt him appear, I raised my right hand. Of course, they thought I'd done something amazing, but the only thing I was guilty of was trying to decide if I was going to climb up the shelves or try to make it to the door if Tiny got loose. Keep watching. Here it comes."

Seltzer and Manning leaned toward the screen, watching as the big dog went from full Cujo to absolute wimp in a matter of seconds.

Manning looked at Jerry. "What'd Gunter do?"

"He didn't do anything. He just appeared. I'm not sure if Tiny actually saw him or just felt his presence, but he was having no part of it."

Seltzer shook his head. "Well, I'll be damned."

Jerry smiled at Manning, who was beaming like a proud papa. "The thing is, we can't let him keep doing things like this."

Both Seltzer and Manning stared at him. It was Seltzer who finally spoke. "We can't?"

"No, it's not fair to the dog. He's lived his life and needs to cross over to the other side."

Manning brushed his hand through his hair. "How do you get him to do that?"

"Not me, you."

"Me? I thought you said he's attached to you."

"Only because I can see him. He needed to come and make sure you were okay. Now that he knows you are – you are, aren't you?"

"I guess. I mean, yes, I am."

"Okay, so now you need to tell him it's time to go."

Manning looked around the room. "Is he here?"

"He is." Jerry pointed to where Gunter sat, intently watching the three of them. "Right over there."

Manning walked to the spot where Jerry indicated. "It's time to cross over now. I'm going to be just fine."

Jerry sighed when the dog looked at him and yawned. "Try it again. A little firmer this time."

"Maybe he doesn't want to go."

I want him to go. "Try it again."

"Okay, Gunter, enough of the heroics. You're off duty. Now go." Manning looked at Jerry, and Jerry smiled. "You mean he's gone?"

Jerry walked over and clamped the man on the shoulder. "You'll not have to worry about him anymore."

"He's gone. I knew it. I felt it the moment he left. He's in a good place now. Happier. I'm glad you let me know he's okay."

"Now I just have to convince the rest of the guys that I'm not crazy."

Manning brightened. "Don't you worry about that. I'll tell them."

"You're a good man, Manning."

"You're not so bad yourself, McNeal."

Seltzer waited for Manning to leave the room before speaking. "The dog's still here, isn't he?"

"Yep."

"Shouldn't it have worked?"

"It did on *The Ghost Whisperer.*"

"Do you know how crazy this all sounds?"

"Yep."

"Now what?"

Jerry looked at the dog, which had once again plastered himself by his side. "I haven't got a clue."

Chapter Eight

Jerry made a beeline for Manning's SUV parked on the far side of the parking lot. Once there, he opened the back door and waited for Gunter to jump inside before slamming the door behind him. With the dog placed in his rightful ride, Jerry hurried to his cruiser, started it, and took off without even giving the car a chance to warm up. As he made a left out of the lot, he glanced in the rearview mirror and saw Gunter's golden-brown eyes staring back at him.

"You know I'm used to working alone, right?" Gunter tilted his head in response. "Listen, Boy, it's not that I have anything against dogs, but the thing is, I've never actually owned one. Given you don't seem to like me, I think it's best if we part ways."

His words prompted a head-tilt in the opposite direction. Not sure what else to say, Jerry concentrated on the road, avoiding the constant impulse to look in the mirror to see if the dog was still there. Not that he had to, as he could feel the dog's presence.

Over the next few hours, Jerry covered the interstate between Carlisle and Greencastle.

Each time he neared Chambersburg, the feeling that something was going to happen intensified. While he didn't know what his senses were picking up, experience told him he still had time to figure it out. He drove around all the area schools and felt certain those were not the intended target.

Just for the heck of it, he drove past Wilson College, happy when his feeling of dread didn't peak. He turned around, then cut through Norland Avenue, making a pass around each of the medical complexes before heading over to Lincoln Highway and stopping at Sheetz for a cup of coffee and hotdog.

The parking lot was full, so he backed into a space near the road and left the car idling, surprised when Gunter seemed content to wait in the cruiser. Jerry headed straight to the coffee station and smiled at an elderly man, who looked up when he neared. The man returned his smile and backed out the way long enough for Jerry to pour himself a cup of black coffee. Jerry recognized the man, who liked his coffee sweet and took his time doctoring it to his satisfaction. Jerry thanked him and went to the kiosk, tapping the screen to order his lunch. He started to complete his transaction, then reconsidered. Though he'd set out some dog food this morning, the dog had refused to eat. Using the back key, he added a second hotdog to his order.

As Jerry stood waiting for them to call his

number, the hair on the back of his neck began to tingle. Instantly on alert, he scanned the store. Several men in business suits stood chatting about a stock they were following. A young man in military fatigues now stood near the coffee station waiting his turn at the counter, while the same older gentleman continued to fumble with his creamers. There were seven open pods on the counter in front of him and three more at the ready. Jerry made eye contact with the younger man and took a sip of his black coffee. The young man smiled and shook his head. While the man fidgeted with impatience, he didn't set off any alarm bells.

Looking in the opposite direction, Jerry saw a young woman wearing a pink puff coat with maroon medical scrubs underneath, pulling several caffeine-laden drinks from behind the glass door of the refrigerator section. The woman looked tired, as if just ending a long shift.

She should be going to bed, so why the need for so much caffeine?

She turned, saw him looking, brushed the hair from her face, and headed for the donut case.

Though Jerry could empathize with the woman, she nor any of the others set off further alarm bells. And yet, the skin on his neck continued to crawl.

Come on, Jerry, you're missing something. Focus.

"Number 51," a voice called from behind the

counter.

Jerry started to walk toward the counter, and the man who'd been fumbling with the creamers cut him off. He waited for the man to hobble out of the way and then moved in to claim his order.

"Have a good day, officer," the brown-eyed girl said, handing him the bag.

As Jerry took it, the feeling of dread dissolved. He turned, making another visual sweep of the area. The two men in suits were gone, as was the woman wearing scrubs. He hurried to the counter in long, determined strides while pulling several singles from his wallet. He handed the woman the ticket along with enough to cover the total with a few pennies left over, then made a beeline for the door.

"Stay safe out there," the woman behind the counter called after him.

Jerry heard the pennies clink in the extra penny tray that sat on the counter and waved a hand over his shoulder in response. The two men he'd seen inside now continued their conversation just outside the door. Jerry made a point of walking near where they were standing, resisting a sigh when his intuition didn't key on either of them. That left the young woman in scrubs, who was nowhere in sight. What he could see was the German shepherd, who'd moved to the front passenger seat in his absence.

"I don't suppose you saw where the woman went," he asked as he slid behind the wheel.

Gunter cocked his head to the side in response. Jerry pulled a hotdog from the bag, unwrapped the foil, and set it on the console. He pulled out the second one, unwrapped it, and took a bite. Gunter licked his lips but made no move to retrieve the hotdog Jerry had placed for him. Jerry nodded toward the hotdog. "Go on, eat."

Gunter bent, sniffed the offering, and promptly disappeared.

Jerry finished his hotdog then, deciding the dog wasn't coming back, ate the other one as well. As he sat drinking his coffee, he thought of the woman who'd set off his inner alarm. While Jerry knew her to be involved, the feeling hadn't been strong enough to consider her the main threat, target, or victim, or whatever his radar was picking up on. Still, he wished he'd been alert enough not to let her slip through his fingers. Following her could have led to the person or persons who would need his help.

He recalled his conversation with Manning and sighed. The man had been right; Jerry was able to pick up on everyone but still not able to save friends. Okay, so technically, the dog wasn't a friend. He looked over his shoulder, half expecting the dog to be there, surprised to feel somewhat disappointed that he wasn't. Manning thought the dog was gone; would it be so bad to let him hang around? *Give it a rest, Jerry. You don't even like dogs.*

Jerry crumpled the foil and tossed it into the

sack. He started to set the bag on the floorboard then changed his mind. Exiting the car, he walked to the front of the building, stepped around the two men who continued to chat despite the frigid air, and tossed the bag in the trash.

"Have a good day," he said, stepping around them for the third time.

"You too," both men replied, confirming what he already knew. Neither of the men had triggered his early warning system. Returning to his police cruiser, he hesitated at seeing a shadow in the backseat. Not only had the dog returned, he was currently lying across the length of the backseat chewing on a meaty bone.

The dog paused from his gnawing, tilting his head as if asking if Jerry were going to stand out in the cold all day.

Jerry looked in the mirror, making eye contact with the dog as he slid behind the wheel. "I don't want to know where you got that. And no blood on the seat; we're already on thin ice with the sergeant."

Gunter licked his lips and went back to chewing on the bone.

Jerry pulled out of his parking spot and drove to the exit debating his next move. The woman had been wearing scrubs. She'd looked tired, but the drink she'd purchased had enough caffeine to keep her awake most of the day. *Maybe she plans to work a double shift. Logical. Okay, hospital or medical office?* Though he'd already made passes around both Chambersburg Hospital and the largest medical complex in town, he decided to give the area another sweep to see if doing so would tweak his inner radar. He turned right and drove the short distance to the hospital. He didn't have to go inside; if the threat had been there, he would have known. He saw the sign that read emergency entrance and thought of Holly.

Focus, Jerry.

Leaving the hospital parking lot, he made his way back to Norland Road; knowing the duration of the drive, he was following the wrong lead. He decided to make another sweep of 81 and started toward Carlisle. Once again, his intuition told him he was going the wrong way, so he pulled into the center median, intending to turn back in the direction he'd just come. Instead of pulling out, he shifted the cruiser into park and sat with his hands pressed together watching the traffic pass. Sitting there served two purposes – it gave him time to clear his mind and slowed traffic – at least until the drivers thought they were out of radar range.

He smiled, knowing the only radar they were on was the one hardwired into his brain. He wondered how the conversation would go if he actually got a hit.

"Sir or madam, step out of your vehicle."

"Is there a problem, officer?"

"Yes, my spider senses told me you're about

to do something awful." He didn't like the term spider – or spidey senses – the names Sergeant Seltzer had given his ability – but he'd never been able to come up with anything better. As it was, none of the cars triggered any feelings, so he decided to take his search elsewhere. He waited for an opening then eased into traffic. The moment he turned back to Chambersburg, he knew he'd made the right decision. He took the Lincoln Highway exit, and Gunter whined.

Jerry looked in the mirror, watching as the dog paced from one side of the car to the other. "Either you need to go to the bathroom or you approve of my choice."

The dog answered with a single bark.

"You let yourself in. I suppose you can let yourself out." Jerry changed lanes then took the Lincoln Highway exit. Having chosen the same exit multiple times, he knew whatever was to take place would occur on or near that highway. He'd no sooner given in to that thought when he saw the banners announcing the psychic convention. Had he missed them before, or had someone just set them out? He decided it was the latter, as surely he would have seen them blowing against the wind. He turned on his turn signal and eased into the parking lot, and instantly knew he'd found what he was searching for.

"Do you feel it too?" Jerry asked when the hairs on the back of his neck began to prickle.

Since he normally worked on his own, it came as a surprise how excited he was to share the feeling with someone – even if the someone in question was a ninety-pound German shepherd no longer of this world. "It's a bit early yet, don't you think? Probably another day, maybe two?"

Gunter paced the backseat, barking his disappointment as Jerry cruised through the parking lot and pulled back onto Lincoln Highway without stopping.

"Nothing's stopping you from getting out," Jerry said when the shepherd turned and looked out the back window, sealing his discontent with a low growl. The dog stayed put, stretching across the backseat to chew on the bone as Jerry turned toward the Borough to make another pass. He drove to the far side of town before circling back and veering his police cruiser into the parking lot across the street from where the psychic convention was to be held. He parked in the rear of the lot, angling so that he could see the main entrance to the building across the street without drawing unwanted attention. The second he put the shifter into park, Gunter materialized onto the passenger side seat, panting so hard, the front windshield began to fog.

"You're a ghost. How can your breath be so warm?"

Gunter curled his lip and growled a soft growl.

Jerry chuckled. "You're offended at being

called a ghost?"

Another growl.

"You do know you're dead, right? I mean, that would explain your walking through walls and disappearing and reappearing in the front seat."

This statement provoked a full snarl.

"Hey, don't be sore at me. I'm not the one that killed you. Okay, full disclosure," Jerry said when the dog tilted his head. "You got shot protecting your partner. You had a grand funeral, and for some reason neither of us has figured out, you came back. Only instead of haunting your former partner, I seem to be stuck with you."

Gunter barked a ferocious bark.

"Okay, okay. For some reason, you've decided I deserve your company. Better?"

Gunter looked at Jerry and licked his lips.

Recalling the bloody bone, Jerry rolled his neck from side to side. "I'm not sure I like that answer."

It wasn't that Jerry didn't like dogs, not really anyway. Saying he didn't like them was a defense mechanism – they were the ones that had built that barrier – running from him – barking whenever he was near and growling when he happened to look in their direction. It had been that way since he was a child. As he sat there staring at the dog, he realized he'd never even gotten close enough to one to feel the softness of their fur. He reached his hand, wondering if it would feel as warm as the breath steaming up the windows. As he neared the dog's head, Gunter whipped around, capturing his hand between his teeth. He gave a warning growl before letting go.

Jerry retracted his hand, nervously inspecting it for tooth marks. "If you don't like me, why are you here?"

The dog cocked his head to the side as if saying, *I've been wondering the same thing myself.*

Chapter Nine

Manning was sitting in his SUV when Jerry arrived at the station at the end of their shift. Seeing Jerry, he climbed out and hurried to greet him. "Is he still gone?"

"Close your eyes."

Manning did as told.

"Do you feel him?"

Manning's brow furrowed then relaxed as he opened his eyes. "No, I think I did it. I helped him find his peace. I think helping him helped me. I've felt so calm today."

"Good deal." Jerry cast a glance at Gunter, who was standing at his side wagging his tail. *At least someone is getting some peace.*

"Maybe that's my new calling. Helping people cross over."

Oh, boy. "I don't think it works like that. I think it worked this time because you had a personal connection to the spirit."

"But it couldn't hurt to try, right? I mean, I don't see them like you do, but if I feel one near, maybe I should tell him it's okay to cross over. That would be alright, don't you think?"

"Sure, Manning."

"Cool. Oh, and I talked to the guys. They were skeptical at first, but then I showed them the tape, and they all saw it too. They think it's pretty cool that Gunter was still on the job. Too bad he had to cross over; we'd make national news. Boy, what a great dog he was." Gunter jumped up on Manning, licking the side of his cheek, and Jerry felt a tinge of jealousy. Manning looked to the sky and brushed away the moisture. "Hey, we'd better get inside; I think it's starting to rain. Glad it held off until the end of our shift."

They walked into the building together, and everyone greeted them with casual indifference. Jerry tossed his hat onto his chair, changed out of his uniform, and headed to Seltzer's office.

"Is he with you?" Sergeant Seltzer asked the moment Jerry entered.

"Joined at the hip."

Seltzer's eyes twinkled. "That must be amazing."

"More like a pain in the ass. I don't know what's worse, him or the cat." *At least the cat seems to like me.*

Seltzer raised an eyebrow. "I never pictured you as a cat guy."

"I'm full of surprises."

"To say the least. Any trouble with the guys?"

"No, apparently, seeing ghosts trumps crazy."

Seltzer chuckled. "Seeing ghosts trumps

86

everything."

"You might want to keep an eye on Manning."

"Is there a problem?"

"I think helping the dog cross was akin to a religious experience. He thinks he has a gift."

"Well, crap."

"Yep."

"You got any preference for patrols tomorrow?"

"I'm going to stay local."

"Your spidey senses tingling?"

Jerry rolled his neck. "Something's brewing."

"Big?"

"I picked up something today. Might be something minor, but whatever it is will need a delicate touch."

Seltzer popped a stick of gum into his mouth and leaned back in his chair. "And you think that's you?"

"Just call me Mr. Finesse."

Seltzer frowned. "Should I bring in more guys?"

"No. I don't think that's necessary."

"You're the boss," Seltzer said, then laughed at the irony.

Jerry knew the risk his boss took each time he allowed him to take the lead on his hunches. Jerry smiled a weak smile. "I'll let you know if anything changes."

Seltzer studied him for a moment. "It's not like you to change before going home."

The man was good. Still, Jerry decided not to share his decision to investigate the psychic convention a bit further. "Thought I'd stop off for a beer."

"You need anything, call my cell." Seltzer hadn't bought the ruse, not that Jerry expected him to.

"Roger that, sir."

"You sure you don't want to tell me where you're going just in case?"

Jerry raised an eyebrow. "So you can have some units in the area? I don't think it's necessary tonight."

"I could order you to tell me."

"I'd lie. Besides, not knowing gives you plausible deniability." Jerry looked at the dog, whose pointed ears had been following the conversation like a beacon. "I'm not going alone."

"Who?"

Jerry jerked his thumb toward Gunter. "He might not like me much, but he seems to be good in a pinch. I have your number on speed dial."

Seltzer looked in the direction of Jerry's hip. "Watch over him, Gunter."

Jerry smiled. He didn't have the heart to tell the man that the dog he was addressing had already moved to the door.

***

Jerry opened the door to his beat-down old Chevy truck, and the dog cut him off, entering with a single leap and moving to the passenger side. Jerry followed him in, sliding behind the wheel and sticking the key into the ignition. He stepped his left foot on the brake, pumping the gas with his right as he turned the key, listening as the engine rolled over a couple of times before sputtering to life. Jerry breathed a sigh of relief then fiddled with the heater, blowing into his hands as he waited for the engine to warm up. He glanced at Gunter, who yawned his disapproval. "You don't approve, find another ride."

Unwavering, the dog licked his lips.

"It's ugly, but it's paid for and dependable, at least most of the time." Jerry pushed on the brake and moved the gearshift into reverse. He crept from the parking lot, then shifted several times as the truck got up to speed. At the end of the road, he geared down, made another left onto Lincoln Highway, shifting and downshifting as traffic warranted. As he drove, Gunter grew restless, whining his aggravation with each delay. Jerry fully understood the dog's frustration and continued down the road as if being led by an invisible guide wire that pulled him toward the building he'd staked out earlier in the day. While the energy pull had escalated, Jerry knew they still had time until the main event.

He backed into a parking space at the far

corner of the lot, then headed toward the building with the dog at his side. He reached for the door then hesitated. "You're not wearing a collar or leash. Maybe you should stay outside."

The dog barked then looked toward the door.

"Okay, but if anyone sees you, I'll deny knowing you." With that, Jerry pulled open the door and walked inside, hesitating momentarily as the energy within the building nearly overloaded his senses.

After several seconds of angst, a sudden calmness washed over him. He looked to see a woman with unnaturally black hair making her way toward him. Despite the weather, she wore open sandals and a multicolored kimono that swept the floor as she walked. Her gaze settled on Gunter and her brows knitted. Her lids lifted with sudden realization, and she visibly swallowed her fear. Jerry instantly knew she was the real deal. Recovering her composure, she smiled broadly, greeting him as one would an old friend. "Welcome. Did you come for a reading?"

I'm not sure why I'm here. Jerry shrugged. "Just thought I'd see what all the fuss is about."

"You've come for answers. I would tell you which tables to avoid," she looked at Gunter once more, "but something tells me you don't need my help with that."

He wasn't sure what to say, so he said nothing.

Unfazed, she licked her painted lips. "Take a

walk around. You'll know when you find what you're looking for – and, officer, thank you for not coming in uniform."

Jerry cocked his head and looked at the woman more closely. It took him a second, but he recognized her as the woman he'd seen wearing scrubs earlier in the day. Sporting heavy make-up, she no longer looked as haggard as she'd appeared when he'd first seen her. The feeling that he'd gotten earlier was no longer linked solely to the woman but more to the building they were standing in. There was more to it, but he knew she was not directly involved with whatever "it" was.

Jerry stood near the opening to the main room, which was alive with excited energy and calming music. Healing drums beat in the distance, luring some in the crowd to the far corner of the room. People of all ages and ethnicity walked about with casual curiosity, inspecting tables covered with crystals, candles, and healing stones. Others sat, desperately holding on to what the medium across the table was telling them. A few held the tepid energy of skeptics – walking around bemused – as if wondering what had led them there. Jerry felt a kinship to those individuals – though he'd been pulled to the space by the "feeling" – he mostly identified with the tepid skeptics, the ones who wanted all the answers but were too cynical to believe anyone capable of delivering them.

He didn't have to enter to find what he was looking for, as the feeling pulled at him like a homing device until, at last, he found himself staring at a young woman who looked to be in her early twenties. She sat at a table close to the door. A stand-up display behind her chair showed a pendulum hovering over a spread-out deck of tarot cards and bold gold lettering introducing her as Mistress Savannah. The write-up underneath her name promised to guide you to what you're looking for, primarily focusing on LOVE, HAPPINESS, and SUCCESS.

Savannah. Jerry wondered if that was the girl's given name or one she'd selected to go with her profession. *It works either way.* The girl emitted an aura of mystery. Round face with even rounder eyes, both deeply shadowed to give her a sultry look, she licked her richly painted lips, pulled another card from the deck, and placed it on the table with the rest.

The man sitting at her table stared straight ahead, making Jerry wonder if he was listening to anything she said. From his puppy-dog infatuated expression, she could just as well be reading from the sports page. It was apparent why he'd chosen her table – the girl was "gifted" in other ways. That she'd chosen to embrace her attributes was evident, as her purple dress showed enough cleavage to allow her to stand out from those not so well-endowed.

Savannah looked up, saw Jerry staring at her,

and smiled a brilliant smile. She slid the tip of her tongue over her lips, batted her long lashes, and motioned him over with a crook of the finger. "I'll be with you shortly," she said, reaching around the man at her table to hand Jerry a business card.

Jerry glanced at the card. *Why go on not knowing about your life? Let Mistress Savannah, healer of the heart, lead you out of the dark.* There was a phone number listed on the back of the card. One look at the number told him it wasn't a local number. Not a surprise, as it was not unusual for conventions to bring in people from out of state. Jerry winked and made a show of tucking the card into his pocket. While he wasn't interested in the girl's thoughts on Love, Happiness, or Success, he was highly interested in why his radar told him she was in trouble – furthermore, the cynical part of him wanted to ask why she didn't already know it.

Deciding to stay inconspicuous, Jerry started walking, thinking to circle the room, intending to slip into the chair once the gentleman that currently occupied it left. He realized Gunter was no longer with him and turned to see the dog sitting beside the table, staring at Savannah with his golden-brown puppy-dog eyes.

Damn, she's good.

Jerry clapped the side of his leg. Gunter's ears twitched, but the dog made no move to join him. He thought to go get him but decided against it. *Not my dog, not my problem.* Besides, the woman hadn't even acknowledged Gunter's presence. *Maybe she can't see him. Perhaps you're the only one that can, Jerry. Not true. Holly not only saw him, she has proof of his existence on her camera. The woman at the door saw him too!* "I'm not the only one."

"Excuse me?"

Jerry turned to see an older woman staring at him. He made a show of removing something from his ear and stuffing it into his pocket. "Sorry, I was on the phone. Bluetooth."

"Oh." The woman smiled, then continued on her way.

Keep it up, Jerry, and they'll have you committed. Just as the thought came to him, a short, stocky man wearing a helmet made entirely of aluminum foil strolled past, muttering to himself. *Great, Jerry McNeal, prior Marine and current Pennsylvania State Trooper, finds himself right at home in a room full of...full of what, Jerry? What makes these people any different than you? You're the one that keeps running away. The guy with the foil might be a complete nutjob, but at least he owns his crazy, not walking through the crowd hiding who he really is. You're the imposter, Jerry. Heck, even the dog is sitting out in the open.*

As the realization hit him, Jerry turned and headed toward the exit. With each step, a voice pulled at him, telling him he hadn't accomplished what he'd come here to do. No, but he was doing something he was good at – running away. He'd run away from home – not in the physical sense – but he'd left as soon as he was old enough to go without being made to return.

He'd run from the Marines – when time and time again, he'd not been able to save his brothers from dying, even though he knew tragedy was about to occur. Manning had been right – he'd even failed to protect the dog. He could have. He'd felt something that morning – a strong pull when he'd seen Manning heading to his SUV with the dog at his side. But it was Manning – something about the guy rubbed him the wrong way, and the dog had paid the price. The thing that haunted Jerry – aside from the dog – was that it could have been Manning that Chambersburg had to bury. In ignoring his so-called gift, had he in some way played God? Was that why the dog decided to haunt him? As penance for not helping his partner?

Just as Jerry reached the door, Gunter barked. Jerry turned and saw the chair in front of Savannah was vacant. She noticed him looking and smiled. In that instant, Jerry knew if he left, he'd be making another fatal mistake. *She's going to die if I don't figure out what is going to happen.*

Jerry turned, retracing his steps. Just before he reached her table, a man cut him off, sinking into the empty chair. As soon as Jerry saw the two together, his feeling of doom escalated to a whole new level.

The dog tilted his head to the side, looking at Jerry as if to say, *You had your chance and blew it. Again.*

Shit.

Chapter Ten

With the two key players identified, Jerry's training took over. While instincts told him to scoop the man up and drag him from the room, the cop in him knew the man hadn't done anything to warrant intervention. Even though Jerry had earned a reputation for knowing when something might happen, the legal system still needed a crime. Telling a judge he had a feeling the man was going to commit a crime would get him nowhere. Besides, while the feeling was strong, it wasn't call-the-cavalry strong. Savannah was safe – at least for the time being.

A man walked past, bumped into Jerry, and mumbled something about him blocking the aisle.

Go easy, Jerry. Stop drawing attention to yourself. You still have plenty of time.

Taking his own advice, Jerry walked to the closest wall, positioning himself so he could see both Savannah and her new client. The man was cleanshaven, appropriately dressed in jeans and jacket, and appeared calm enough. Unlike the previous man, this guy actually seemed to be staring at the girl's face and not her breasts.

Savannah slid a credit card reader across the table, waited for her client to insert his card, then pulled the reader out of his reach, simultaneously pushing the button on a small timer and turning it for him to see. So far, everything seemed above board.

Savannah chatted with the man for a moment, then shuffled the tarot cards, placing them onto the table in groups of three. Still chatting with the man, she lifted a card, frowned, then instantly covered with the same brilliant smile she'd used on Jerry earlier. If the man had noticed the fleeting frown, he didn't let on. Instead, he tapped a second card. Savannah lifted the card, sucked in a breath of air, then returned it to the table without comment. Still talking to the man, she snuck a peek at the last card. Her expression remained nonplussed as she gathered the cards and placed them to the side without explanation. The man looked at the table, a frown creasing his forehead. The frown lessened the instant Savannah took his hand in hers.

She flipped the hand so she could see his palm, studied it briefly, then pointed something out with the index finger of her right hand. Whatever she told him must have resonated, as his shoulders relaxed. He said something to her, and she pointed to his palm once more. Savannah seemed slightly more at ease now, though her smile still seemed a bit forced. She chatted with the man for several more moments before lifting her hands, as if telling him that was all. As if to firm her point, she pressed the button on the timer and pulled his card from the reader, handing it over to him. He stood, returned the card to his wallet, and left. Unlike others who continued to walk through the room, the man headed straight for the door. As he neared, Jerry went into cop mode, making a mental note of the man's description – brown hair, hazel eyes, and a faded scar just over the guy's left eyebrow. He also noted red clay on the edge of the guy's work boot and used the doorframe to gauge his height as he exited the room. Though the guy was smiling when he left, the feeling of unease hovered over him like a dark raincloud as he left.

Jerry thought about following him, but experience told him there was no need. Whatever was going to happen was going to take place on these premises. Soon, but not tonight. While he still didn't know what it was, he knew it would involve the mysterious Savannah.

Jerry pushed off the wall, walked to Savannah's table, and claimed the empty chair.

"I'm sorry about before," she said, glancing toward the door. "I thought about telling the guy you were next, but I wasn't sure if you were actually interested in a reading or just hanging around for the view."

Jerry smiled, keeping his eyes above her neckline. "You're a lovely young lady."

She cocked her head to the side. "I detect a

'but' in there."

"But…you're not my type."

She smiled. "And yet here you are."

"Here I am," Jerry agreed.

Savannah slid the card reader across the table, waited for Jerry to insert his card, then pressed the timer as she'd done with her previous client. Pulling the card reader out of reach, she turned her palms up, sweeping them across the table. "So, what will it be, cards or palm?"

"How about I let you decide?"

"Cards it is." She picked up the tarot deck and began shuffling. "Ask the cards your question as I'm shuffling. What will it be: Love, Happiness, or Success?"

Jerry shrugged. "Why don't we let the cards decide what they want me to know?"

"Suit yourself." After a moment, she stopped shuffling and dealt them onto the table in three separate piles. After placing the final card onto the center pile, she lifted her gaze to him. "Pick three in any order."

Jerry studied the deck for a moment, then tapped the center pile, the one to the left, and lastly, tapped a finger on the card to the right.

Savannah hesitated for a moment before turning over the middle card. Once she did, she let out an audible sigh then turned the other two over in order. "If that isn't a clear message, I don't know what is."

Jerry looked at the cards. "All I see is a

shepherd in a flowing white robe, a man driving a chariot, and a man holding a wand."

Savannah laughed a carefree laugh. "That's why you're paying me to interpret for you."

Also known as throwing money out the window. Jerry resisted voicing that aloud as she pointed to the first card.

"The Hermit signifies a journey." She motioned to the card with the chariot. "This also signifies a journey. Care to guess what this one means?"

Jerry looked at the card with the man holding the wand. "That you're going to wave your magic wand and send me away?"

"Not me, but it's the King of Wands, which shows the journey could begin at any moment. Are you planning on taking a trip?"

Jerry thought to tell her he'd been moments from fleeing when his conscience made him come back, but decided against it. "Nope."

She frowned and mumbled something under her breath.

"Excuse me?"

"What? Oh, nothing." She scooped the cards into a pile, set them aside, and reached for his hand. "I'm much better at reading palms."

Jerry raised a brow. "I couldn't help notice you had trouble with the last gentleman who occupied this chair."

Savannah's mouth fell open, and she narrowed her eyes. "You were watching?"

"Waiting my turn," Jerry corrected.

"Invading a man's privacy's more like it," she said sharply.

Too sharply – leading Jerry to believe she was more embarrassed she'd been caught than worried about privacy in a place where anyone walking past a table couldn't help but overhear what was said. Intuition told him the conversation they'd had was pivotal, so he decided to press the issue. "I couldn't help notice his cards seemed to upset you."

She remained quiet for a good moment as if debating her answer, then lowered her voice. "The man gave me the creeps the moment he sat down. Then when I turned the cards over…"

"Bad?"

She closed her eyes for a moment rubbing her arms with her hands. "To say the least. The Devil, the Tower, and Death."

They're just cards. Jerry fought to keep the cynicism from his voice. "Sounds bad."

"The worst."

"Couldn't have been too bad. The man was smiling when he left."

She looked around once more. "That's because I lied."

The hairs on Jerry's neck prickled. "That doesn't sound very ethical."

She laughed. "I'm not a doctor."

"No, but people come to you for advice." This time, he let his anger show.

She shrugged. "I gave him advice."

"Just not the advice he needed to hear."

"You know I charge by the minute, right? I mean, I don't mind idle chit-chat, but this isn't a date. While you're sitting in that chair, it's your dime."

"Hooker wages." She blushed, and he instantly regretted his words.

Instead of shrinking away from his words, she pulled herself taller in the chair. "I can think of worse ways to make a living. And I might show a bit of cleavage, but I like to think of it as window dressing. How many times have you browsed through a catalog knowing good and well you couldn't afford what was inside the cover?" She raised a hand and motioned around the room. "There are many tables to choose from, and I'm the youngest reader in the room. I know why men sit in my chair – that's why I dress the way I do. But it stops at this table. Oh, sure, I've had men offer me more if I were to leave with them, but I've never taken any of them up on their offer. I'm not that kind of a girl."

Are you trying to convince yourself or me? Jerry smiled a disarming smile. "So, what did you tell the man?"

She sighed. "What are you, a cop or something?"

He thought about telling her about his feeling, but something told him she wouldn't believe him any more than he believed her. "Just trying to figure out why a man who'd pulled such a bad hand left the building walking like he'd won the lottery."

"Aside from the view?" She winked, then leaned in and lowered her voice once more. "Listen, I did the guy a favor. He told me he was tired of living in a dump and wanted to see if he'd be moving anytime soon."

"Too bad he didn't draw my hand."

"Too bad. Listen, if I had told him what his cards really said, he would have freaked out. I've seen it happen. The guy would've probably stayed all night, and it would've cost him a fortune." She glanced at the credit card reader and winked. "I hope you have a good job."

The state will pay for this one. "So you did him a favor. What happens when he finds out you lied?"

She leaned back in her chair. "The convention's over tomorrow. I'll be long gone by the time his luck changes."

Doubtful. "And if you're not?"

"Then I'll tell him I made a mistake."

It was Jerry's turn to sigh. "I hope you didn't make a bigger mistake than you bargained for."

Her face turned serious. "Do you think he's dangerous?"

The last thing Jerry wanted to do was escalate the situation. "I think he's a guy. Sometimes guys do things without thinking them through."

She held her hand out, and he offered her his

palm. She shook her head. "No, I'd like something personal."

"My hands are attached to my person."

"Your watch. I'm not going to steal it," she said when he hesitated.

Jerry slipped the watch off and handed it to her, shifting in his seat as she wrapped her fingers around it and closed her eyes. A frown tugged at her lips, and he resisted the urge to demand she return it.

When at last she opened her eyes, they were brimming with tears. "You hold on to a lot of pain."

You have no idea. Jerry forced a smile. "I'm in the prime of my life."

"I'm not talking physical pain, and you know it."

Lucky guess. Even still, he thought about snatching the watch and making a beeline for the door.

"I didn't read the cards right."

For a moment, he wondered if she meant his or the man before him. He got his answer when next she spoke.

"You're not going on a trip. You're running away."

He reached for his watch, and she pulled it back, keeping it just out of his reach. "You've done it before. You're always seeking answers for things you don't understand, and when you don't get the answers you want, you run away."

This was more than just a lucky guess. Jerry struggled to keep his voice even. "I'll take my watch back now."

"You'll never get the answers you seek if you keep running." She looked him in the eye. "Your friends' deaths are not your fault."

Jerry pushed from his chair, all pretense of remaining calm forgotten. "Give me my watch."

She stood keeping her fingers closed. "I understand why you were afraid to get your own reading. What I don't understand is why you came here in the first place."

Because I was stupid enough to think this was all a bunch of smoke and mirrors. "Do me a favor. You see that man come through those doors, get up and go to the bathroom. Hide behind a table or go out the back door."

Her eyebrows knitted together. "You know something you're not telling me."

Jerry laughed at the irony. "You're the medium. Figure it out."

She opened her hand, letting the watch fall into his open palm. "Mr. McNeal?" she called as he turned to leave.

Jerry hesitated. He hadn't given her his name. *Max picked up on Holly's name sounding like Christmas.* He turned, thinking to ask her how she'd zeroed in on his precise name.

"Forgot your credit card," she said, holding it for him to see.

Jerry took the card, feeling instantly relieved.

Savannah hadn't read him; she'd guessed. *Good job, Jerry; you fed her the information she needed.* Shaking his head at the misstep, he pocketed the credit card with a Marine corps emblem on it. *Then how'd she known about the running away? Another lucky guess.*

She called his name again, and he turned for a second time. Before he could ask what she wanted, she nodded to the side of the table where Gunter was lying with his muzzle resting on his front paws. "Don't forget to take your dog."

"I don't have a dog," Jerry said, bolting for the door.

Chapter Eleven

Jerry rushed from the building, the only thing on his mind getting as far away as possible. Not just from the building but away from things he couldn't control. Women that knew too much about his thoughts and dogs who could appear and disappear at will. He didn't stop to consider the logic of running from a dog who could move between realms, not that it mattered, since he was in no state of mind to listen to logic – not that there was anything logical about ghosts.

The truck started on the first turn, and Jerry sped out of the parking lot with no destination in mind. His decisions were made on a clear path – if the traffic light was green, he continued in that direction. If red, he turned. He stopped at a stop sign, saw a car to his right, and turned left, following the path of least resistance. He drove, staring straight ahead with both hands on the wheel, only removing his right to shift gears. Sweat beaded on his forehead and his heart raced so fast, he wondered if he was having more than a panic attack. Though he knew what set him off, all he kept thinking was what if. What if – this time it was real? What if – they found him in a field after having run off the road because this time he was actually having the heart attack he'd imagined so many times before? That was all his life seemed to be anymore: a perpetual game of what-ifs.

It wasn't until he was nearly to the Mason-Dixon line that the panic ebbed, and he became rational enough to pull to the side of the road. He sat there for several moments, flexing his fingers, which ached from gripping the steering wheel, rolled his neck from side to side to relieve the tension, and took in his surroundings as he waited for his heart rate to return to normal.

Jerry saw movement to his left, looked out the window, and saw a long line of black cows standing near the fence, each stretching their neck over the wire as if to see what was going on. Jerry wondered if they were welcoming him or hoping he'd come bearing food. Either way, having them standing nearby was a tad comforting. If he were still on the brink of panic, they would have picked up on it and stayed clear.

It had been some time since he'd experienced an anxiety attack of this magnitude, and he was glad he wasn't on duty. They'd take away his gun. The last thing he wanted was to be stuck at a desk job for the rest of his career. *Get your shit together, Jerry!*

Jerry dug his cell phone from his pocket, found the number he was looking for, and hit dial.

The call was answered on the third ring. "McNeal, talk to me, buddy."

Jerry struggled to keep his voice casual. "Hey, Doc, how's it going?"

Laughter drifted from the phone. "Working hard, drinking harder."

That Doc was drinking didn't come as a surprise; that he'd mentioned it made the hair on the back of Jerry's neck tingle. "Anything I need to be worried about?"

"Not until I start mixing the two. I start drinking on the job, then I've got trouble." Doc was the Navy Corpsman who'd been assigned to Jerry's Marine unit and, as such, had made two trips into Bagdad with Jerry and the others. While most of the unit had gotten out when their enlistment was over, Doc was still serving. Instead of being in the field, he'd advanced to the rank of Chief and was currently stationed in Maryland at the Bethesda Navy Hospital just outside of DC.

"Heard from any of the others?"

"Boz, Turner, and Delong."

"Everything cool?"

"Nothing a few moments on the phone with me couldn't cure."

Though the man on the other end couldn't see him, Jerry nodded his understanding. In turn, Doc had approached each man in the unit, making them promise that if they ever needed to talk, they would give him a call. He was so dedicated to that quest, he'd purchased a separate satellite phone so that he'd never miss any of their calls. Turner had told Jerry that Doc once answered his call, even though he'd been in a closed meeting with his commanding officer at the time. When Jerry had asked Doc if it was true, he'd confirmed, saying he'd gotten himself out of being court-martialed by giving the CO his private number to give to the man's son, also a Marine, serving in a different unit.

"How are things in PA?" Doc asked after a moment.

"Good." It was a lie, and both men knew it. Still, even though Doc knew the reason for the call, he never asked for details unless Jerry brought it up. It wasn't the first time Jerry had phoned his lifeline. Just hearing the man's voice was enough. It wasn't about what was said or not said, it was about knowing someone was there. After hearing the Chief's voice, Jerry was feeling calm enough to be embarrassed to have needed him in the first place. "Listen, I've got to be going."

"Doing some of that cop shit?"

"Something like that."

"You cool, Jerry?"

"Better than," Jerry said, ending the call. He gripped the phone, picturing the man's face. *Thank you.* Why he couldn't say the words directly to the man, he didn't know. Maybe because doing so would show Doc how vulnerable he really was. Calling on the pretense of a casual phone call was one thing. Letting on that he'd had another panic attack was another. Putting the truck into gear, Jerry turned the wheel and headed back toward Chambersburg.

***

While he was feeling better, Jerry had no desire to go home. Craving breakfast, he headed for the Waffle House, pleased when he pulled up to the building, looked through the windows, and saw an empty booth. As he entered, he made eye contact with his regular waitress. Tall and thin, Roxy had worked there for as long as Jerry had lived in the area. Though she knew Jerry was a state trooper, she never gave away his secret when he was out of uniform.

"The usual?" she asked, setting silverware and black coffee on the table in front of him.

Jerry nodded and wrapped his hands around the cup. Now that he was out of the truck, he allowed his mind to wander, trying to pinpoint what exactly had set off this latest panic attack. Savannah told him he'd be running away. Yes, but there was more to it. She'd touched on the fact that he hadn't been able to save his friends. She'd said he wasn't responsible, as if saying it would make it true. But he was there, had felt something about to happen, and yet he wasn't able to prevent it. *Not his fault – tell it to the men who died.*

"Need a top-off?"

Jerry looked to see Roxy standing next to him, holding a coffee pot. He started to hand her his cup then realized he'd yet to take a drink. "I'm good at the moment."

"Your food will be out shortly," she said, walking away.

Jerry felt a blast of cold air, looked toward the door, and sighed. Savannah and the woman he'd seen wearing scrubs were standing in the doorway searching for a place to sit.

Jerry scanned the room, hoping to see an empty table. There were none.

The ladies looked in his direction, their gaze settling on him.

Shit!

The unnamed woman smiled, stepped in his direction, and Savannah grabbed hold of her arm, pulling her back. Jerry was about to sigh his relief, when his arm went up, seemingly on its own, waving them over. *Double shit. Why, Jerry?* Before he could answer his own question, the woman pulled her arm free and walked the short distance to his booth.

"Mind if we join you?"

Yes. Jerry swiped his hand to the opposite side. "Be my guest."

"Thanks," she said, sliding across the bench.

Though her body language told him she'd prefer not to, Savannah joined them, sitting beside her friend.

"Thank you for sharing your table. I've been

craving breakfast all day. I'm Raven, by the way, and this is Savannah, but I believe you two have already met. She said she scared you off. Ow!" she said when Savannah jabbed her with her elbow. "What? That's what you said."

"And yet, you wish to humiliate me more by making me sit with him?"

"Jerry McNeal." He looked at Savannah. "Why, pray tell, would you be humiliated for giving me a reading?"

Cassidy waved a hand to summon the waitress then looked at Jerry. "She's new, so she didn't know how to react when you ran off. You went out the door, and she ran to the bathroom. I wasn't sure what had happened until I went in and found her sobbing her head off."

"That's enough, Cassidy," Savannah said through gritted teeth.

"Okay, now I've really done it. She's using her mom voice, calling me by my real name. We're sisters, in case you can't tell."

"Which is why she was able to con me into coming up for the convention," Savannah explained. "Cassidy told me she was lonely and wanted some company. The next thing I know, she's sticking me in a dress a size too small and telling me to read the cards."

Roxy came to drop off Jerry's plate and gave the girls a once over. By the set of her jaw, Jerry could see she disapproved of how they were dressed. "Can I get you two… ladies something to eat?"

"I'll have what he's having," Cassidy said, studying Jerry's plate of smothered and covered hashbrowns with scrambled eggs.

Savannah wrinkled her nose. "I'll have scrambled eggs, bacon, crispy hashbrowns, and white toast."

"And to drink?"

"Large orange juice," both girls said at once.

"That looks so good. I'm starving," Cassidy said when Jerry picked up his fork.

Jerry set his fork aside and pushed his plate across the table. "Go ahead. I can wait."

Cassidy pulled the plate closer and started in on the food without apology. She took a bite and moaned her approval.

Savannah rolled her eyes. "Really, Cass?"

"What? I worked all night and most of the day covering another shift and worked as hostess at the convention. I'm starving."

"That explains the monster drink."

Cassidy stopped chewing and looked at him. "God, was that this morning? It's been a long day."

"I don't know why you didn't let me play hostess. You're better at the cards than I am."

"You know what you're doing. That's why you agreed to come in the first place. You've just got to build up your confidence with the cards."

"Maybe I could be more confident if you quit dressing me like a whore."

For a moment, Jerry wondered if they'd forgotten he was there. Roxy came to the table to drop off the orange juices, saw Cassidy eating Jerry's meal, and shook her head.

Jerry looked at Roxy and shrugged. "She was hungry."

"She's something," Roxy grumbled.

Cassidy grabbed Roxy's arm, studied her palm, and winked. "You're no saint yourself."

Roxy pulled her hand away and left without a word.

Jerry looked at her over his coffee cup. "You know you shouldn't piss off the people who handle your food."

Cassidy fired off another wink. "I've already got my food."

"Touché." Jerry turned his attention to Savannah. "So, what made you want to be a psychic?"

"It was her idea."

"She's got the gift. We both do, even though she doesn't always believe it. Our mom and grandmother have it. Or had – our grandmother's dead."

"I've heard it can sometimes skip a generation. Or come on without any family ties." Jerry tried to make his questions sound random. While he had the gift, his mother did not. His grandmother did some of what she'd referred to as conjuring, but his brother hadn't had the gift.

"I guess it can be either way. Are you the only

one in your family who has the gift?"

Savannah's mouth dropped open. "You have the gift?"

"Of course he does. Don't tell me you didn't pick up on it."

Savannah blushed. "No, the guy before him threw me off. By the time Jerry sat down, all I could get from him was he was a nonbeliever."

"Is it true that you don't believe?" Cassidy sat her fork on her plate and laughed when Jerry shrugged.

Roxy brought the remaining plates. "Anything else?" Everyone shook their head, and she placed the food on the table and left.

Cassidy smiled at Jerry. "I see my little sister isn't the only one who needs to learn to embrace their gift."

"That ship sailed a long time ago."

"Okay, so you believe. So what? Do you think you're the only one with intuition?"

"I think there are a lot of frauds out there." He nodded toward Savannah. "I also think if you go around giving people bad advice, it could come back to haunt you."

Cassidy smiled. "Speaking of which, where's your dog?"

"I have no clue. The last time I saw him, he was with your sister."

Savannah's eyes flew open. "I don't have him. I turned my head, and when I looked back, he was gone. I thought he went looking for you.

I hope he didn't go out on his own; he's liable to get killed. You don't think someone stole him, do you?"

Cassidy looked at Jerry and smiled a sly smile. "Do you want to tell her, or should I?"

Jerry lifted his coffee cup and gave her a nod. "You better do it. She's not going to believe me."

Chapter Twelve

Garrett Lutz, a man of many titles – husband, father, liar – was sitting on a house of cards, so flimsy one misstep, and he would lose everything. A few short months ago, he was on top of the world, with a beautiful wife, a new baby daughter, and a job offer that allowed him to be home every night to help with the baby. It also held the promise of moving his precious family out of the dump in which they currently lived.

The dream job had lasted precisely one week – that was how long it took his new employer to discover Garrett had lied about having a college degree. Why they'd waited until after hiring him to do an in-depth background check was beyond him. A simple computer check could have saved them all a lot of heartache, and he'd still have his job at the warehouse. While it wasn't his dream job, it had kept the roof over his family's head and allowed him to stick money into savings each month – savings that were nearly gone, as he'd been using it to pay the bills since his termination.

Termination – he could think of a few people

he'd like to terminate.

Garrett opened the briefcase his wife Rene had surprised him with on the first day of his new job and pulled out a notebook. Maybe if he made a list of everyone who'd done him wrong, it would help calm his nerves. He clicked the pen and wrote the name, Patrick Menendez. The man who'd taken great pleasure in telling him he was fired and pointing toward the door like a parent sending a child to the corner. Boy, had that pissed him off – especially since everyone was watching. Menendez further humiliated him when he crossed his arms like a bodyguard and wouldn't let Garrett explain to the boss why he'd falsified his resume. If only Menendez would've allowed him into the man's office to show him the photo he'd taken on his camera phone the night before, this could have all been sorted out. The photo, showing the tears of joy in his wife's eyes when she'd pulled up some new home listings, would melt anyone's heart. It certainly had warmed his. They'd spent the next few hours making a wish list of all the things they wanted for their new home. He couldn't remember the last time he'd seen her that happy. She'd had such a rough go of it as of late. Postpartum. The doctors promised it would be temporary. He couldn't bear to add to her sadness, which was why he refused to tell her the truth, at least not until he had a replacement job under his belt.

Garrett searched his mind for another name.

Pam. He didn't know her last name, but that was okay – he knew where she worked. He looked about the room, surprised to see her looking directly at him. He hated her. Loathed the way she'd told him he wasn't allowed to take up a table unless he was a paying customer. Hated that she'd cost him a small fortune in fancy coffee drinks over the past three months. You don't treat a person like that, especially not one that's in your place of business eight hours a day. He lifted his cup, took a drink, and smiled as she turned away.

Garrett used the pen to write another name: Shockley. Now there was a man he'd like to terminate. How dare Shockley refuse to give him his old job back. The man knew how desperate he was, especially since Garrett had explained everything. Yeah, he'd sure like to terminate Shockley.

Using the pen, he wrote another name: Garrett Lutz. Garrett stared at the name – his name – as if thinking of someone else. *Now there's a man that needs terminating. For a smart man, he sure is dumb.* Taking a bad situation and making it worse by not being honest with his wife. How stupid of him to have dipped into what little savings they had to pay the bills while sitting in the coffee shop all day using his laptop to look for work. He could've easily found a job – hell, even the coffee shop he used as his office had a sign in the window. But he refused to lower his standards. *Yeah, that guy sure needs terminating.*

Garrett shook his head to clear it and lined out his name. He was being too hard on himself. Any man in his situation would've done the same thing if they'd seen the look of hope on Rene's face when she'd learned of the promised paid vacations, health insurance, and a whole host of other things. Rene immediately pulled out her phone to call her mother to tell her the news. She'd then asked if it would be alright to purchase a few things. Unable to tell her no, he'd laughed and told her to spend away, as their income had more than doubled.

Garrett couldn't bear to tell her he'd screwed up again. So he didn't. He continued to set his alarm, pretended to go to work, then came home each day and listened to her tell him how proud she was of him. And each day, their savings dwindled a little more. He'd cringe when she told him she'd used her credit card to purchase a little something new for the house or the baby. It wasn't her fault; she'd never been frivolous with money before, and since he paid the bills, she had no idea how precarious their situation was. If only he'd told her the truth, then he might not be in this mess, but he hadn't, and no amount of wishing he had was going to change that. Everything was going to be okay. He just needed a bit of time.

His hand shook as he prepared to press send

on yet another resume, a job he was qualified for in every way except for the lack of the same degree that had gotten him fired before. Still, he'd faked it before; he might get away with it again. He had the experience – he'd been working warehouse jobs for years. He'd even filled in for his boss a time or two.

Garrett pounded his fist on the table, startling a couple sitting next to him. He was glad Shockley hadn't taken him back. The last thing he wanted was to start at the bottom again. The bottom meant third shift, and he'd promised Rene he would be there to help with Lydia when she woke during the night. He needed days, and he needed enough money to buy his wife that beautiful new house she dreamed of. She deserved it. They deserved it. It had worked before and would work again – it had to.

***

Garrett pulled into the driveway, his heart clenching when he saw Rene standing in the front window holding the baby. The little woman waiting for her provider to come home, only he wasn't a provider; he was a deadbeat. A knot formed in the pit of his stomach, and he struggled to contain the self-loathing as he gathered his briefcase and headed to the house, continuing the charade he'd started weeks ago.

Rene failed to smile when he entered. He set his briefcase on the table and turned to her, saw her trembling, and for a moment, thought there was something wrong with the baby. He was just about to ask, when his wife spoke.

"Where have you been?"

"What do you mean? You know I've been at work."

She narrowed her beautiful eyes. "Liar."

She knew. He didn't know how she knew, but she did. Still, she could be upset at something else. "Excuse me?"

"You don't have a job. You've been lying to me all this time."

"How'd you find out?"

Tears brimmed her eyes. "We got the results from the radium test today. It was positive. I called to see how much it was to have the basement sealed. I wanted to surprise you by taking care of it since you've been working so hard. I gave them my credit card number, and it was declined. I thought there'd been a mistake, so I signed in to the account to check. Garrett, we are nearly broke!"

"I can explain."

"You don't have to. I tried to call you, and your phone went to voice mail, so I called the number you gave me for your office. The man who answered said you got fired months ago."

Garrett reached into his pocket, pulled out his cell phone, pushed a couple of buttons, and got nothing. "It's dead. I must have forgotten to charge it."

She hugged the baby tighter. "That's all you

have to say to me?"

"For now. You're upset. It wouldn't do any good to try and explain myself right now."

"You're damn right I'm upset. Where do you go every day, and what have you been spending our money on?"

Garrett sighed. This was the ugly side of his wife – the one he preferred not to see. He walked to the table, plugged in his phone, and waited until there was enough power to turn it back on before answering. "There was a little problem with my job, and I didn't want to stress you out. You were already on edge with the baby and all. Not to worry; I've been looking for a new job. I'm not going back to my old one either. We both know I'm much too smart to take a pay cut."

She stared at him for a moment before speaking. "You're unemployed. I'm pretty sure anything would be better than that."

"I'm not going to accept anything less than a management position. Something will come along soon; just you wait and see." Actually, he was glad she found out. Now he could stop pretending. Plus, it would save money not paying for all that coffee. He thought of the list and wondered if he should remove Pam's name.

The baby started to fuss, and Rene bounced her in her arms. "What are we going to do about the radium? I'll not have Lydia exposed to that."

He started to ask her how much it would cost to fix and decided against it. Obviously, there wasn't enough left in the account, or they wouldn't be having this discussion. "I'll fix it myself."

"You?"

He didn't like the way she'd spat the word – as if she didn't think him capable of keeping her and Lydia safe. "Yes, me. See, there's an upside to my not working. If I was, we'd have to pay someone to take care of it. As it is, I have plenty of time to do it myself."

Lydia started to cry, and Garrett decided to let Rene tend to her while he went to change out of his suit. By the time he returned, Rene was sitting in the rocker nursing Lydia. He'd never truly appreciated the task before but was suddenly thankful they didn't have the added burden of purchasing formula. That was the thing about his wife; she could be frugal when she needed to, and with his secret out, they'd have to find creative ways to stretch what money they had left until he landed another job.

Garrett pulled on his old coat, picked up the flashlight, and went to take a look around the house. Truth be told, he hadn't a clue what he was doing, but Rene didn't know that. All he had to do was poke around some and pretend to take care of the issue. It would take weeks to order another test and wait for the results. By then, he'd be working and would have enough money to pay to have it fixed – at least until it was time to move to a better house.

Garrett trudged through the snow, aiming the flashlight at the foundation until he came to a spot where the snow had drifted away. He kicked at the dirt with the toe of his work boot, grimacing when he hit the red clay. He wasn't going to convince Rene it was fixed if he couldn't show her where he'd dug.

He made his way back to the front door, opened it, and stuck in his head. "I'm going to town to get a shovel. Do you need anything?"

She shook her head without answering. The baby must have fallen asleep. He started to leave, then went back to the door, stepping inside, mindless of the mess he was leaving, and collected her car keys from the table.

Garrett was on his way to the hardware store when he saw the signs announcing the psychic convention. He'd never had his fortune read and felt a bit silly spending money so frivolously, but he needed some assurance that everything was going to be okay. A chair opened up at a table close to the door, and he decided it was a sign. To his surprise, the moment he sat down, the girl slid a credit card reader in front of him. He didn't want to look like a cheapskate, so he inserted his card, hoping it wouldn't get rejected. When it went through, he considered it another sign that the beautiful girl in front of him would show him the way.

Chapter Thirteen

Jerry arrived at work early, anxious to speak with Seltzer, only to find his sergeant in a closed-door meeting with the captain. Unable to relax, Jerry walked a path between the coffeepot and his cubicle – walking the route so much, even Gunter grew tired of following and lay on the floor beside Jerry's chair with his head resting on his front paws. Though the dog didn't follow, he continued to watch Jerry's every move.

Several of the guys came in, Manning among them. Seeing Jerry, he said something to the others and joined him at the coffee station. "McNeal, you're in early."

Jerry forced a smile. "Yep."

"Who's the sergeant in with?"

"The captain."

A sly smile appeared on Manning's face, and he quickly covered it by lifting an eyebrow. "Awful early for him to come by."

Tell me about it. "Yep."

"You're a man of few words, huh, McNeal."

Only when I don't like you. Instead of answering, Jerry just stared at the guy.

Manning shrugged. "Where are you

patrolling today?"

"I'm staying local."

"I thought you were local yesterday."

"I was." Jerry knew some of the guys took exception to his special liberties. But Seltzer always managed to smooth them over – at least until now. The second Manning mentioned it, Jerry's intuition told him that was precisely what they were discussing in the other room. *Please don't let it be an issue. Not today.*

Manning leaned in and lowered his voice. "I might have overheard some of the guys talking. I think someone might have gone over the sergeant's head."

Jerry tightened his grip on his coffee cup. "Geez, I wonder who that could be?"

Manning threw up his hands. "Not me, bro; you and I are pals. We've got a connection now since we can both do the same thing. As a matter of fact, I planned on talking to the sergeant about that very thing. I've got a hunch that something big is going to happen around here soon. No, today. Definitely today."

Jerry looked toward the dog and willed him to hear his words. *Bite him.* He sighed when the dog failed to respond. He turned his attention back to Manning, who looked past him to where Gunter lay on the floor.

"Whatcha looking at, Jerry?"

Trying to see where you'd land if I clubbed you with this cup. "Just thinking about grabbing my cover and getting on the road."

Manning didn't buy his answer, and it showed. Before Jerry could say anything, Seltzer's door opened, and the sergeant stuck his head out and waved him over.

Shit.

"Kick the door around." He waited for Jerry to close the door before continuing. "The captain has had a complaint. It seems someone thinks I've been giving you special privileges."

Jerry looked at the captain. "Someone?"

The captain nodded. "Anonymous."

"Anyway, the captain here feels you need to do some farther patrols and let some of the other guys stay local for a bit."

"Okay, but not today."

The captain's head jerked up. "Excuse me? Who's in charge here?"

"You two are, but today, I need to stay local." He wanted to add that his spidey senses were sending shockwaves throughout his body but didn't think sharing that would help his case. At least not with the captain.

Seltzer knew Jerry well enough to know why Jerry had bucked at the change and nodded his agreement. "Very well; local it is."

The captain looked between the two. "That is not what we discussed."

Seltzer held firm. "What we discussed was for future scheduling. I already have Jerry patrolling Chambersburg today."

"Then switch him."

Jerry looked at Seltzer and shook his head.

Seltzer held firm. "The schedule stays the way it is today. Any changes will be on next week's schedule. That will be all, Trooper McNeal."

Jerry hesitated. He'd hoped to talk to Seltzer alone and fill him in with what little details he knew.

"I said you may leave, McNeal."

"Yes, sir." *Shit. I can't let him take the heat for this.* Jerry faced the captain. "Sir, I'm not sure what the sergeant here has told you, but I have a gift. The sergeant calls it my spidey sense, but whatever it is, I can sometimes see things before they happen."

"So I've heard." The captain didn't sound convinced.

"Something is going to happen here today, and I need to be here to make sure innocent people don't die."

"So why not just tell your sergeant what's going to take place and let him send some troopers?"

"It doesn't work that way. I'm led to where I'm needed." Okay, so that was only a minor lie. He did know where it was going to happen. But he also knew he was the one that needed to defuse the situation so others didn't get hurt.

Indecision pulled at the captain's face. "Why you, McNeal?"

Jerry sighed. "Sir, I ask myself that same thing each and every day."

The captain stood. "You have it your way today, trooper, but things in this department will change, and we will run this post by the book. And for what it's worth, I wish you luck with whatever you think is going to happen."

Still hoping to have a word with the sergeant, Jerry stepped to the side.

The captain looked over his shoulder. "I think I'll stay in town for a while today just in case you need anything."

The moment he left, Sergeant Seltzer reached into his drawer and pulled out a pack of gum. "Well, that was fun."

Jerry chuckled. "I can think of other words for it."

"Ah, no worries. I needed to lose a few pounds. I haven't had an ass-chewing like that in a long time. Any idea who anonymous is?"

Jerry gave a nod to Manning, who was in the outer room talking to the captain. "A pretty good one."

Seltzer stood and looked out his inner office window. "Manning? I thought the two of you found some common ground."

"Too common."

"How so?"

"I'd make a wager he's telling the captain he has a feeling something big is going down today."

Seltzer raised an eyebrow. "How'd he come by that information?"

"Guessed it when I told him I was planning on staying local."

"The captain is going to think I'm running a loony bin. No offense."

Jerry laughed once more. "None taken. Hey, about today. I know the where and also have an idea who the key players are."

"Give me the names, and I'll have them brought in."

"You know it doesn't work that way. You saw the captain. The only reason he agreed to it today is my track record. No crime, no arrest. Something's going to happen at the psychic convention. I'm going to drive my pickup. I can't get close enough in the cruiser. I'm not sure when – probably a few hours yet. They don't let people in until nine."

"Okay, you know how it works – you need us – we'll be there."

Jerry smiled. "That's what I'm counting on."

***

Jerry parked in the same space he'd had the previous day. Backed in and hunkered in the seat, he had a clear view of the front door. Not that it mattered, as Gunter was sitting in the seat beside him, pointed ears turning like radar antennas. Jerry nodded toward the door. "Can you feel it? Not much longer."

Gunter woofed his agreement.

Several moments later, Gunter growled. Jerry looked and heaved a heavy sigh as a State Police SUV pulled into the parking lot and backed in beside him.

Manning lowered his window, and Jerry resisted the sudden urge to shoot the man. "What the hell are you doing here?"

"I followed my instincts, and they led me here."

Jerry was tired of playing nice. Things were going to go down soon, and he didn't need to be babysitting. "That's a load of crap, and you know it. You saw my truck. Now get out of here before it's too late."

Instead of leaving, Manning closed his window.

"Jesus, how did you ever...." Realizing the dog was no longer in the truck, he stopped without finishing his sentence. *Okay, dog, why'd you leave?* His spidey senses were on full alert as he searched the parking lot. *Come on, Jerry, concentrate.* Jerry's cell rang, causing Jerry to jump.

"McNeal? Why the hell haven't you called?"

"Excuse me?"

"The sheriff's department just got a call about a nut job with a knife at the psychic convention."

Shit! "Manning!"

"Manning's got a knife?"

"No, he distracted me. I've got to go." Jerry saw Manning getting out of his cruiser and ended the call. "Manning, where do you think you're going?"

"Inside. Didn't you get the call? Every cop in the county is on the way."

"You're not going in."

"Last time I checked, you weren't the boss."

Think, Jerry. A chill ran the length of him, and Jerry saw Manning lying on the floor in a pool of blood. "You can't go in. If you do, you'll be killed."

"Killed?"

I'm sure of it. "That's right, remember when you accused me of not knowing when something was going to happen to my friends? You were right. But this time, I know, and that's why I can't let you go in."

"We're friends?"

Not really. "Yes, and that's why you need to stay out here and control the situation. Don't let anyone inside unless I request them. Can you do that, buddy? I'm counting on you."

"Go on, McNeal. I've got your back."

Jerry drew his pistol and quietly made his way inside the building. A crowd of onlookers stood close to the man as he wielded a knife and screamed obscenities. *They're too close. He could stab any one of them before I get to him.* Jerry closed the distance while keeping an eye on the blade. *Knife?* It didn't make sense; the vision showed Manning with a bullet wound. Jerry hoped he wouldn't have to drop the man but knew he might not have a choice.

As Jerry approached, Cassidy saw him and caught her breath. He wanted to ask where her sister was, but there was no time as the suspect raised the knife in Jerry's direction. Training told Jerry to fire, but instinct told him to wait. While the man was clearly in distress, Jerry knew he was not the person the guy wished to harm.

Keeping his pistol trained on the guy, Jerry raised his left hand. "Put the knife down."

"I can't." The man's voice cracked as he spoke.

"Sure you can. Just lower your arm."

"Where's the girl?"

Jerry kept his eyes on the knife, the blade glistening against the bright overhead lights with every move. *Play along, Jerry.* "What girl?"

"The freaking psychic!" the man screamed.

Keep the focus, Jerry. He'd allowed himself to get distracted once. He'd not let it happen again. "Is there someone in particular you're hoping to find?"

"She was here last night, but I can't find her now."

"Maybe she has the day off." Not likely, but it would explain Savannah's absence from the table.

"It's a two-day convention. They don't take days off. She's here, I know it. She knows what she did and is hiding from me."

As if to prove his point, the tablecloth moved,

and Jerry knew Savannah was hiding under the table. *Don't do anything stupid, kid; he doesn't know you're there.*

Jerry took a step closer, keeping his pistol trained on the man's chest. "What's your name?"

"My name is back the freak off!" the man yelled in response.

Easy, Jerry. Taking his own advice, Jerry planted in place, squaring his knees. "I'm not going to be able to do that, sir. Just tell me your name, and I'll help you figure out where she is."

The man hesitated a moment before answering, "Garrett."

"Garrett, you got a last name?"

"No way, man. I'm not stupid – I give you my last name, and you can do that cop shit. You ain't got no reason to know my full name."

"Just trying to get to know you, sir."

Garrett grabbed his crotch. "Yeah, get to know this."

Jerry could hear sirens in the distance. *Come on, Manning, I'm counting on you.* He'd no sooner keyed on the man than he again saw him lying in a pool of blood—*not going to happen.* Jerry reached up, carefully opening his mike for others to hear. "Come on, man. Right now, it's just you and me – there's no reason to get anyone else involved. In a few moments, the whole district will be here. That happens, and things can get messy. You don't want that. You just want to find your girl."

"She ain't my girl. She's nothing to me."

Easy, Jerry. "Why didn't you say so? You don't need a knife to talk to one of these pretty ladies. I'm sure any of them will be more than happy to give you a free reading."

"I don't want a freaking reading! What do you think started all of this to begin with?"

Jerry kept his voice calm. "That's what I am trying to figure out. I'm trying to help, Garrett. We get this misunderstanding cleared up, and we can all go home tonight."

Garrett lowered the knife. It was only a slight dip, but they were heading in the right direction. "I can't go home. My old lady took the baby and left me this morning. It don't make any sense, dude. I was in here yesterday and told the woman I was tired of living in a dump. I told her I'd applied for a new job, and the woman – this Savannah – was like, I know, I can see it. You're going places. She said not to worry, that I would be moving to new digs real soon."

Jerry had to give it to Savannah – she was right on that aspect. Garrett would be moving to the county jail as soon as it was safe to handcuff him. Jerry spoke clearly, hoping to let the other units know he was making progress. "What do you say you lower that knife some more, and we go find this girl together. We'll have her give you a new reading and ask her what the mix-up was. I'm pretty sure when she finds out how much she missed the mark, she'll give you a refund from yesterday. You can use the money, right?"

Garrett lowered his arm another notch. "Yeah...yes, I can. That shit ain't right. She didn't say anything about my wife leaving me or this here today. You know what I think?"

That she lied to you? "No, dude, tell me what you think."

"I think she saw me losing my wife, and she wanted me to come back here for another reading so she could tell me what I am supposed to do now."

If the situation weren't so dire, Jerry would have laughed. "I'll tell you what, you lower the knife, and I'll pay for today's reading myself."

"For real, dude?"

Geez, the poor son of a gun actually believes me. "For real. You drop the knife, and I'll see to it personally."

Just as Garrett started to lower the knife, Jerry heard a noise behind him. Someone said something about them sending in another cop, and Jerry felt more than knew that Manning was on his way inside. Garrett reached for his waistband, and Jerry saw the handle of a pistol.

Shit!

Jerry's finger was on the trigger when he caught sight of brown and black fur sailing past in a single leap. Garrett screamed and fired. Gunter disappeared just as Garrett slammed into Savannah's table. "Suspect down! I repeat, the suspect is down!"

Jerry jammed his pistol into its holster, kicked the knife and gun away, and pulled out his cuffs. He clamped them onto Garrett's wrists as he reached up and turned off his mike.

"Where is he?" Garrett's voice was a panic.

You killed him. Don't be ridiculous, Jerry. The dog's already dead. "Where's who?"

"The dog, man. I didn't see him until he was flying through the air."

Savannah peeked out from under the table, and Jerry saw tears rolling down her cheeks.

Speaking low, Jerry whispered in Garrett's ear, "You want to know your future, here it is. There was no dog. It was a ghost. How else would you explain the way he disappeared? Ask anyone here, and they'll deny seeing it. Don't believe me, have your lawyer request the video from the cameras. The other officers are coming in now. Tell them you were trying to give me the gun, and it accidentally went off. Get yourself a good lawyer who can get you help for the demons inside your mind. But heed my words, you bother that girl or anyone else ever again, and that dog will find you and rip out your heart. Trust me on this."

Jerry pulled Garrett to his feet and handed him off to a local officer. As the cop led him away, Jerry reached a hand to help Savannah from under the table.

Her hands shook as she batted tears from her face. She kept her words to a whisper. "I heard what you said to him, but he's right. Your dog grabbed hold of my arm and pulled me from the chair a second before the guy came in. I was getting ready to call for help when I saw him. I remembered what you said and hid under the table."

Before Jerry could answer, Manning joined them, his face pale. "It didn't sound like the guy was listening, and I wanted to help. I saw him pull the gun and dove for cover as he took the shot. Seriously, Jerry, he was aiming right for me. I don't know how he missed. I guess I must have a guardian angel watching over me."

Jerry looked about the room, disappointed when he didn't see Gunter. He made eye contact with Savannah and Manning in turn. "I'd say you both had an angel looking out for you today."

Chapter Fourteen

Jerry woke from a nightmare, looked at the clock, and groaned. Two forty in the morning on a day he wasn't scheduled to work. He closed his eyes, replaying the dream in his head for several moments before finally deciding he wasn't going back to sleep. Opening his eyes once more, he realized Cat was staring at him from the pillow next to his head. "What are you doing here, Cat?"

He got his answer an instant later when he felt the dog's presence and turned to find Gunter standing next to him, the dog's head even with Jerry's face. It was Gunter's first appearance since the incident at the convention, and Jerry found himself glad to see him. He reached his hand toward the dog and Gunter growled.

Jerry recoiled, Cat hissed and took off running, and Gunter gave chase. Jerry pulled himself up, sitting on the side of the bed and trying to pinpoint the precise moment when his life had become a cartoon.

Deciding to let the animals sort things out for themselves, he dressed for his morning run. The moment he opened the door, Gunter bolted down the stairs in front of him, bouncing around in the snow like an eager puppy.

"You'd better not let Wells see you." As the words left his mouth, he realized that though the dog was racing through the yard, he wasn't leaving any pawprints behind. Nor were there any new yellow marks in the freshly fallen snow. Maybe Gunter wasn't so bad after all.

Jerry rolled his neck and took off in a slow jog. After allowing his leg muscles to warm, he increased his pace, running along the snowy street, oblivious of the biting air.

As he ran, the shepherd raced along at his side. Jerry couldn't help but wonder if the dog were chasing some unseen demon – or running away like he was. He usually loved running on mornings like this, enjoying the peacefulness of the freshly fallen snow, as if the white blanket somehow created a barrier from the ugliness in the world. But not today – this morning, he ran from dreams he could not shake and decisions that needed to be made. Should he renew his lease? Doing so would mean another three-year commitment, and as such, would be the longest he'd remained in one place since reaching adulthood. He liked his job well enough, but wasn't sure he could deal with the new restrictions. It was the same thing that had helped make his decision to leave the Marine Corps; his instincts would tell him to go one way, and his commanding officers would send him another.

The captain had made it clear that he would

not receive any special treatment. If the sergeant didn't follow those orders, it would likely mean the end of the man's career. Not a problem if Jerry could agree to the new rules, but he couldn't, not when lives were at stake. If he hadn't been there yesterday, people would have gotten killed.

Are you sure, Jerry? It's not like it was you who stopped the guy from shooting Manning. Is that why Gunter returned? To save his old partner? There had to be more to it than that. Jerry slowed his pace and finally stopped walking altogether. Gunter circled back around and stood watching him. "Manning's safe. Why are you still here?"

Gunter barked his answer.

"I don't understand."

Gunter barked once more, and Jerry's frustration grew. It was just like in the dream he'd had with Joseph standing in the fog trying to show him something he couldn't see. In his dream, the fog had lifted, and their grandmother was standing there mouthing words he couldn't understand. Jerry told her so, and she'd looked at him with sad brown eyes similar to the ones staring at him right now. Gunter took a step forward and then another until he was standing close enough for Jerry to touch. Jerry crouched, staring the dog directly in the eye. *What do you want from me, dog?* Jerry reached a hand toward Gunter. As he did, the cell phone in his pocket rang. Jerry jumped and Gunter disappeared. Jerry sighed his frustration as he answered the phone. "You're calling early."

"That's because I got called early. One of those ladies from the psychic convention called and tried to convince me to give her your phone number – said she has something for you."

"What'd you tell her?"

"I told her it was against policy and that I'd pass along the message, so consider it passed. Oh, she told me to tell you it was kind of urgent."

"Did she leave a number?"

"Nope. She said something about being hungry and that you'd know where to find her."

Jerry smiled and started for his apartment. "Anything else?"

"Not from her, but I got a call from Chambersburg PD. Seems our guy lawyered up, and his attorney wants the video from the cameras. It's pretty soon for the request; anything on there I need to be concerned about?"

"Nothing that's going to help him."

"That's what I wanted to hear. PD still hasn't found the bullet – they plan to give it another go today."

"They won't find it." Jerry replayed the scene in his head, his stomach clenching when the bullet entered the dog. If not for Gunter, Manning would have been shot and Holly would have died. His intuition led him to both places, and yet it was the dog who'd saved the day both times. *Then why was I there?*

"Are you still there, McNeal?"

"I'm here."

"You did good in there yesterday. Turns out the guy's a real nutjob. PD found a hit list in his briefcase. The girl must have really upset him, as he moved her name to the top of the list. I don't know how that radar of yours works, but it was really on point with this one. I wish I could tell you I was able to smooth things over with the captain, but he's determined to run this post by the books. You'd think he'd see things differently after yesterday."

That was the thing – nothing happened that should have changed anyone's mind. Jerry had allowed himself to get distracted. If not for that, he would have seen Garrett enter and had reasonable cause to search and disarm him. As it was, he was just a Pennsylvania State Trooper doing his job. "The captain's just doing his job, Sergeant. At the end of the day, that's all any of us can do."

"That's a load of manure, and you know it. Manning told me you warned him not to go inside, said that was the only reason he ducked when he saw the gun. You might not want to admit it, but you saved the man's life."

Jerry started into his driveway and saw Wells standing on the stairwell to his apartment. "Shit. I got to go."

"Something wrong?"

"Nothing I can't handle." Jerry clicked off the phone, intending to have it out with Wells. Instead, he found himself getting into his truck and driving away just as Wells made it to the bottom of the steps. He was still trying to figure out why he felt the need to avoid speaking to the guy when he stopped a block down the road to clean the snow from his windshield.

***

Jerry stepped inside the Waffle House and saw Savannah sitting in the same booth they'd shared with her sister two days earlier. Dressed much more conservatively in a purple sweater and simple makeup, she lowered her cell phone and motioned him over the moment she saw him. "I see you got my message."

"It appears so." He raised an eyebrow when the waitress approached the table with his usual order along with a cup of black coffee.

"I took the liberty of ordering for you. Day off?"

Jerry looked at his sweats. "Does it show?"

"A little."

He took a sip of the coffee, grateful for its warmth. "My sergeant said you have something for me."

Savannah lowered her fork and blew out a long breath. "More like a message."

Instantly on alert, Jerry mirrored her actions.

"He spoke to me yesterday when you took my hand, but I didn't have a chance to tell you."

"This should be good."

"I know you're not a believer, but your brother says he's been trying to reach you."

Joseph? The dream. Jerry struggled to keep all emotion from his face. "Say I was to believe you. Just what is it my brother wants me to know?"

Another sigh. "I'm not sure what it means, but he wants me to tell you to stop being cheap."

Jerry laughed. "That sounds like him."

"Do you understand the message?"

"You mean that's it? Is this your way of getting me to pay for breakfast?"

"No, of course not. I owe you more than breakfast for saving my life."

"But we both know I wasn't the one who saved it."

She stared at him, unblinking. "What do you mean? If not for you, I'd be sitting at my table when the guy came back. I wouldn't have known anything was wrong, and he would've probably stabbed me, shot me, or both."

No doubt. "But it was the dog who did the saving."

"He wants to know why you don't like him."

"You're going to sit there and tell me you're talking to my brother right now?"

She pointed her thumb toward the floor. "Not unless your brother has four legs and a tail."

Jerry looked to where she was pointing and saw Gunter staring up at him. He rolled his neck to relieve the tension. "Nice try."

"What?"

"We both know you can see him. That doesn't mean you can talk to him, much less understand him."

She ignored his comment. "It's one of my gifts. He was sent here to help you, and you keep trying to send him away."

"Sent here by who?"

"Your brother."

"Doubtful. He knows I don't like dogs."

"He says you told him the only reason you don't like them is because they don't like you."

Jerry's mouth went dry. If his brother was here, why couldn't he see or feel him? "Joseph's here?"

"He just showed up."

It was getting a bit too crowded in the small diner. Jerry looked to the door.

"She doesn't want you to go."

The woman was all over the place. "You can't even keep your own story straight. He, she, the dog."

"Was your grandmother very religious?"

Granny's here too? He snickered into his coffee cup. "Only on Sunday."

"She said to watch your manners."

Now that sounds like Granny.

"She's mad at you."

Missed the mark again, lady. "I was her favorite."

"Wait – I can't understand when you're both speaking."

"I think I'll be going." Jerry started to leave and found himself unable to move. "What the hell?"

"I think your brother is playing tricks on you. Are you sure your grandmother wasn't religious?"

He didn't want to believe, but something – or someone – was keeping him from leaving. "Why do you think she's religious?"

"Just a phrase she keeps repeating. Jesus, Mary, and Joseph."

Jerry laughed a hearty laugh. "That's not what she's saying. My brother's name was Joseph. Anytime the two of us started carrying on, she would always scold us by saying, 'Jesus, Jerry and Joseph, behave yourselves.'"

Savannah bit at her bottom lip. "So you believe me now?"

Kind of hard not to. Jerry nodded, then frowned. "I've seen spirits before. Why can't I see or feel them?"

"I don't know. Maybe they didn't think you'd listen to them."

"You said she's mad at me?"

"She's upset you're driving her truck."

"She left it to me."

"Only because she didn't know what else to do with it. Your brother's saying you're driving it because you're cheap. He said to spend some of the money he left you to get a new one, and your grandmother is echoing his words."

"Tell him he didn't leave me any money; it was his life insurance policy."

"Same thing." She held out a hand as if to silence someone. "They both say you are not living up to your potential. They don't like the way you keep beating yourself up when you don't get the results you want. They think you need help and said that's why they sent you the dog."

Jerry blinked his surprise. "They sent him?"

"Yes, to help you. They said you shouldn't have to do this on your own."

"Do what?"

"Fight crime."

"I'm not sure I can do this anymore."

"This what? Talking to your family?"

He shook his head. "Being a cop."

"You're not happy with the state police?"

"I'm not happy period."

"You're not thinking?"

"Of killing myself? No. It wouldn't do any good anyway, since I'd probably be like the dog and come back as a ghost. At least now I get to eat real food."

"When I did your reading, I picked up that you'd be running away. It seemed to be cut and dry. I felt you'd done the same thing before."

"I have."

"What if I read you wrong?"

"Doubtful; that's my MO. I run when things get bad."

"Are things bad now?"

"Not bad, just confusing. I feel like a fraud."

"Oh, you're the real deal, alright."

"Not with this. With the police department. I feel like I don't belong. I ride around following my feelings. It's rare that I do any real police work, and it's not only me. I put my sergeant at risk every time I go out." *Shut up, Jerry.*

"You're conflicted."

"You think?"

"So why fight it? Maybe you should go." She smiled. "They're agreeing with me."

"I thought you weren't supposed to tell people what they wanted to hear?"

"I'm not. I'm totally serious. It's only a matter of time before something happens to make you leave anyway. So why not leave on your own terms? You regret your decision to leave the Marines because you ran away. Running away as you did and leaving things unfinished makes you feel like a coward. We both know it isn't true, but it doesn't keep it from nagging at you, especially when things aren't going well on the outside. If you leave the State Police on a whim, it will be another nail in your already fragile inner infrastructure. Wouldn't it be best for all involved – especially you – to leave while you're on an upward curve? You leave on good terms; they would be more apt to take you back or put in a good word at another department should you ever decide you're ready to return."

"Is this you talking, or them?"

Another smile. "A little of all of us, I think."

They had a point. Jerry rolled his neck once more. "I'm not sure if I just had a reading or a counseling session."

"Does it matter?"

"Only because I think I need to fire my counselor." He smiled. "Do you do phone readings?"

"I've never tried, but I think it's worth a try if you ever need me. So, does that mean you're going to take my...our advice?"

"It means you've given me a lot to think about. Although I'm not sure what I'm supposed to do about Cat."

"The dog said the cat must go." She shrugged. "I like cats. I'll take him."

"You've never even met him."

"It doesn't matter. He's a cat. Cats are cool."

He liked her. A lot. He looked at her wedding ring. "Your husband is a lucky man."

"Wife."

"Excuse me?"

"My wife is a lucky lady."

He shook his head. "I didn't see that coming."

She winked. "That's why I get paid the big bucks."

"Because you married a woman?"

She laughed an easy laugh. "Because I can see things most can't. Mr. McNeal?"

"What happened to Jerry?"

"Okay, Jerry. I think you're overthinking things."

"What things."

"With the dog."

"How so?"

"You're trying to treat him like a dog."

"Okay."

"No, I mean, it's obvious he's a dog. But he's a spirit first and foremost."

"So that's why they sent him to me?"

"They may have sent him, but he had to play some part in it. I think it's more like he chose you."

"Why would he do that when he could have picked Manning or anyone else on the planet?"

"Manning would have treated him like a dog. I think he chose you because you're more like him. You feel things." She held up her hand before he could object. "I think he knows what your purpose is on earth, and he's here to help guide you."

"How can he know my purpose when I don't know?"

"He will help you."

"You mean like Lassie?"

She looked at Gunter and shook her head. "I'd say more like Rin Tin Tin."

***

Wells was sitting at Jerry's table when he entered. He had a copy of Jerry's lease in front of him and drummed it with his index finger. "Before you go touting laws on trespassing, I'll have you remember I gave you notice."

Jerry walked to the table, pulled the lease from under the man's finger, scribbled on the paper, and handed it back to him. "No, Mr. Wells, it is I who's giving you notice. I will be out of here by the end of the month."

Wells studied the paper as if expecting the ink to disappear. "Leaving. What a shame. I'll hate to see you go."

Jerry resisted the urge to toss the man out by the seat of his pants. "If we've nothing more to discuss…"

Wells took the hint and hurried out the door, which Jerry locked behind the man. As he wrenched the deadbolt, it felt like a weight had suddenly lifted from his shoulders. When he turned, he saw Gunter staring at him.

"She said you were sent here to show me the way. I'm cool with you hanging around if you are."

Gunter answered with a single bark.

Jerry laughed a carefree laugh. "If we are going to be partners, we're going to have to work on our communication skills."

Taking a chance, Jerry kneeled.

Gunter took a tentative step and then another until he reached Jerry, pushing his forehead into

Jerry's chest. Jerry moved slowly, raking his fingers through the dog's black and tan coat, enjoying the softness of the K-9's surprisingly warm fur. In that moment, Jerry felt a peace he'd never felt before.

Ghostly Guidance

*Join Jerry McNeal and his ghostly
K-9 partner as they put their gifts to good
use in:*

Rambling Spirit
Book 3 in the Jerry McNeal series.

*Available March 18, 2022 on Amazon
Kindle*

Please help me by leaving a review!

About the Author

Born in Kentucky, Sherry got her start in writing by pledging to write a happy ending to a good friend who was going through some really tough times. The story surprised her by taking over and practically writing itself. What started off as a way to make her friend smile started her on a journey that would forever change her life. Sherry readily admits to hearing voices and is convinced that being married to her best friend for forty-one-plus years goes a long way in helping her write happily-ever-afters.

Sherry resides in Michigan and spends most of her time writing from her home office, traveling to book signing events, and giving lectures on the Orphan Trains.

Made in the USA
Las Vegas, NV
09 December 2023

82363091R00095